SENSATION

Bailey stepped up to Sam as soon as he hung up the telephone. "You sounded angry. What gives?"

Excited about the lead in Earl's case, Sam hauled Bailey flat against his chest. She felt good, real good. "A tip about last night."

A dozen alarms rang through Bailey's mind. "You're kidding! Who called?"

"Elsie Goddard."

Bailey searched her practical mind of past catering clients and events. "I've never heard of her. What did she say to you?"

After Sam repeated the conversation, Bailey was indignant. "She called you angel? I don't like it."

"Her calling me angel or her calling me instead of the police?"

"Both, and I'm not being jealous."

Sam leaned the hard muscles of his behind against the counter, ankles crossed, arms akimbo. His dark eyes tracked Bailey's every step. "I know. If these were normal circumstances I would never have listened to the woman for as long as I did. I listened to her because I want to see those punks nailed. That's why I agreed to meet her."

LOOK FOR THESE ARABESQUE ROMANCES

WHISPERED PROMISES   (0-7860-0307-3, $4.99)
by Brenda Jackson

AGAINST ALL ODDS   (0-7860-0308-1, $4.99)
by Gwynn Forster

ALL FOR LOVE   (0-7860-0309-X, $4.99)
by Raynetta Manees

ONLY HERS   (0-7860-0255-7, $4.99)
by Francis Ray

HOME SWEET HOME   (0-7860-0276-X, $4.99)
by Rochelle Alers

SENSATION

Shelby Lewis

Pinnacle Books
Kensington Publishing Corp.
http://www.pinnaclebooks.com

PINNACLE BOOKS are published by

Kensington Publishing Corp.
850 Third Avenue
New York, NY 10022

First Printing: January, 1997
10 9 8 7 6 5 4 3 2 1

Printed in the United States of America

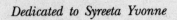

Dedicated to Syreeta Yvonne

Sometimes, it's like a hair across your cheek. You can't see it, you can't find it with your fingers, but you keep brushing at it because the feel of it is irritating.

—Marian Anderson, regarding racism

Friday

Skeletons at the Feast

One

In his middle thirties, Sam Walker cut a striking figure. Ebony skinned, broad shouldered, and densely built, he left the convenience store with two iced teas tucked under his arm in a brown paper bag, his attention arrested by a neatly dressed teenaged boy. It was 9:00 P.M.

The teen quickly crossed the store's parking lot, an old Thunderbird nearly running him down. Aware that something was terribly wrong, Sam studied the offending car. Its engine rattled, in need of repair. Its dull metal exterior required fresh paint and a new coat of wax. The car's dirty front grill lacked a license plate. The teen looked scared.

Calculating quickly, Sam saw the car carried five skinheads: two women, three men, each one of them yelling obscenities into the hot, late August air. Loud, abrasive rock music exploded from the battered car, slamming against the cracked pavement beneath Sam's feet.

Alarmed, he watched as the dirty car doors swung open on the Thunderbird, its pale-skinned riders screaming hateful, shocking words at the dredlocked teen. The three skinhead males carried baseball bats: two aluminum, one wood.

The men converged upon their teen victim. The victim's face was solemn, his body lithe, his stance limber beneath a red and white-striped cotton shirt, which fit snugly in the band of his dark navy jeans. He looked all-American; healthy, strong, well groomed with classic features.

His own body tight with worry, Sam ticked off the boy's limited options: the skinheads were strong, in their late teens or early twenties, they carried weapons, and the boy was unarmed.

Decisively, Sam returned his jumble of keys to his pants pocket, placed his brown paper bag on the pavement, then readied himself to defend the young stranger.

The tallest male opponent glowered at him for interrupting. "Step aside," the steely man warned, his voice rigid, controlled. He raised his wooden baseball bat in a threatening gesture to make Sam cower. The gesture failed.

Sam glared at him, his strong jaw clenched, his big hands fisted, his hard thighs coiled. "No." He was committed.

Gripping the ends of his bat with both hands, the scowling foe shoved Sam roughly across his chest before muttering, "Fine." The other skinheads said, "Yeah," in agreement. His legs spread wide of his long body, Sam pushed the man back. The fight was on.

Bats flying, two skinhead males peeled away from their watching women to knock him to the dirty pavement. He rolled to the right, away from a steel-toed boot poised to kick him in the chest. Sam leapt to his feet, the scene deadly.

The skinhead males stormed their intended victim like dogs tracking a bone. They repeatedly pounded the fallen teen, a boy who blocked the fatal blows as best he could, a boy who refused to scream or beg anyone for mercy.

The teen's courage boosted Sam's efforts to win as he rammed a foe in the back with his shoulder, a harsh fighting move that sent the hapless skinhead sailing deep into the dark green juniper that crept across the only landscaped area near the convenience store. The skinhead roared.

A second opponent raised his bat with both hands in retaliation, aiming the hard weapon at Sam's vulnerable spine. One swift second before contact, Sam twisted his long body safely away.

Besides the cashier, there were two other witnesses to the hate crime: a woman leaving Starla's with a pizza in her hands and an old man leaving the convenience store with a newspaper under his arm.

The cashier called the police. The woman slammed the pizza box on a skinhead's back. The skinhead swung around to face her. She ducked his baseball bat and kicked him in the leg. He swung again. The old man pushed her aside to take the blow. The blow landed on his thigh.

The cashier locked the convenience store, stuffed his keys in his pocket and helped the old man. Together they pulled two skinheads off the teen. Sam threw his body into the remaining skinhead; they fell into the skinhead women, knocking one of them down.

Distant police sirens zeroed in on the fight. The teen lay on the ground, unmoving. The cashier and the old man kept at it. Sam wrestled the bat from his green-eyed foe. The men fought blow for blow, will for will, hate for hate. The woman, now without the pizza, ran to Starla's for more help.

"Get him, Bash!" Sam heard the skinhead women cry, women too caught up in the moment's thrill to worry about the outcome of their violence. "That's it, Grip! Harder, Snake!"

Sam's ears logged the names the young, misguided women so carelessly shouted, identifying the names for later police reference: *Bash, Grip, Snake.* They were young men, corrupt men.

As police sirens wailed closer to the gang beating, the two skinhead women ran to the Thunderbird. With her long hair flying, the brunette resumed her spot in the driver's seat of the still running car. The blonde jumped in the passenger side, shouting, "Let's go! Let's go!"

The skinhead men pulled back and got into the car. More help came from Starla's Pizza Parlor, but too late. In a flash, the gang plummeted into traffic; disappearing into the hot August night shouting a string of abrasive, warlike rebel yells. The police missed the skinheads by seconds.

Gently, reverently, Sam cradled the fallen, badly beaten boy. All his life Sam had believed in God's mercy. Holding the boy's broken body against his chest, he questioned God's love. At that moment, he did not know what kind of God would allow a child to have such terrible pain. Sam was angry.

But then the boy stirred gently in his arms, a small miraculous movement that salvaged Sam's tarnished faith. The boy's lashes, long and ginger-colored, fought the gravity that pulled him down into a black bottomless hole, a mystical space in God's great universe.

A gifted student of the universe, the boy knew all about black holes, the one place in the cosmos where gravity pulled with such force that no power, not even light, escaped its divine strength.

Unable to open his eyes, the boy tried to move his lips, tried to tell Sam he feared nothing in the black hole, a thing made when a star drained its light and heat to build a supernova, a blast so strong it crumbled other stars into minuscule dots.

Slowly, painfully, the boy opened his swelling eyes, their lashes fluttering as he battled the invisible weight that pulled him ever downward into eternity. The boy's eyes were blue, not just any blue, but sapphire blue; eyes that gleamed with tears into the night.

Sam leaned close as the dying child spoke to him, his voice so incredibly soft he nearly missed it. The child's lips brushed his ear as he murmured, "Thank you." Sam's gut wrenched.

The instant he spoke, the boy relaxed his shattered body and something beautiful burst like a supernova inside his deepest self. In theory, the boy's shattered body devolved into organ systems, a spiritual death. His organs split into molecules, the molecules split into atoms.

The atoms soared along the winds of light into outer space, the true keeper of the young boy's dreams. This surreal blast rocked his core to create a lasting break between his body, his mind, and his soul. His physical coil split open to seed the earth.

This spiritual tearing down of the victim's body created a truly fresh, truly limitless being, a heavenly being made of pure energy. For the victim, this physical death broke him away from known worldly boundaries so that the unknown universe was now possible; for him, this was Nirvana.

In shock, Sam watched as ginger-colored lashes eased down, slowly and completely, over sapphire-blue eyes. Sam's powerful muscles trembled as the body he held stopped twitching beneath golden-shaded skin. Slender lips, though broken, fell open in a smile as the young boy freed his last breath.

As if on cue, two burly policemen approached Sam's bowed form. With them, they brought order, a civil, lawful way to manage the chaos created by the racist hate crime, a crime that shocked the predominantly black neighborhood.

Sam watched the men come, knowing they could not help him find peace after being the prime witness to the end of a young man's life. Holding the victim to his chest, Sam wept.

Two

Homicide Detective Ridge Williams arrived at Jasper Mini Mart as a police crew were gathering vital evidence of the crime. News of the hate crime shot through the middle-class neighborhood like brush fire, burning residents with racial tension. This tension worried the detective. His brow furrowed with premonitions of evil.

The people of New Hope neighborhood were incensed. The detective feared that once the residents found out where the skinheads came from, youths of the neighborhood area would hunt the gang down, destroying property in the process.

Though he understood that any rioting done would be based on a common sense of kinship, the detective believed that more violence had to be stopped at any cost. For this reason, he and his police friends would have to work quickly in order to solve the crime.

Cutting a dashing figure with his commanding stance, Ridge's dark eyes skimmed the emergency crew for Carlyle Higgins, a buff colored man with a light brown afro and hazel eyes. The detective in charge of the crime scene, Carlyle stuttered slightly, a speech impediment Ridge seldom noticed anymore. The men worked well together.

Carlyle managed the command post, the center of all supervised police activity, a job Ridge thought he did well, another reason why the men worked superbly together. Each man was a master in his area of expertise.

From the command post, Carlyle directed men to secure photographs and videotape of the crime scene. He appointed officers to crowd control. He supervised the search for physical evidence. Above all, he made sure the murder victim stayed protected until his initial exam by a medical official. Ridge followed through with the details.

Relieved to see the detective, Carlyle met Ridge with a solid handshake, a firm gesture of shared respect and civic duty. They were special friends, men united by honor, integrity, and power.

"The first uniformed officer here, Leroy Douglas, secured the area with t-t-tape," Carlyle said, releasing his grip. Both men knew that securing the area was urgent when protecting a crime scene from contamination.

"Good."

Carlyle flicked hazel eyes across his small pad of field investigation notes. Dressed in light brown slacks, tan shirt, and silk tie he looked every bit the professional. "There are witnesses to all or part of the b-b-beating. I'm getting names, addresses, and phone numbers."

Methodically, Ridge clicked deeper into detective mode, the state of mind he used to weigh facts, the disconnected particles of news that helped him dissect truth from fiction, a vital aspect of his challenging job.

When he gleaned the truth about the skinhead beating, he needed it to be without bias. If he failed to curb bias within himself, he would fail when it came to dealing with the varied prejudices of witnesses to the crimes he investigated: the families of victims, and ultimately the suspects themselves. He believed people were innocent until proven guilty in a court of law.

For Ridge, anything other than an objective use of his time marred his integrity as a police officer. It reduced him to the level of vigilante, someone self-appointed to

private causes rather than to the good of the many, which
he was sworn by law to protect.

The hour was late and he was tired. The muscles in his
lower back ached with fatigue. When the call came about
the murder, he was elbow-deep in routine paperwork; report writing, filing, and answering mail.

He knew that anyone connected to the beating, via
something seen, heard, or experienced was key to the fast
capture of suspects. "I'll go over the results with you tomorrow morning in my office," he said. By then, the first
step in solving the hate crime would be finished: the initial
gathering of on site evidence.

Though Saturday was not his scheduled day to come
into the office at the police station, Carlyle agreed to come
because he took his duties seriously. Like Ridge, he wanted
to avoid more harm to the neighborhood's morale. "Then
I'd best get c-c-cracking."

As Ridge walked away from Carlyle, energy-sapping heat
washed over him. His short-sleeved shirt stuck to his skin,
as did the triple-pleated slacks that tapered neatly to the
tops of his leather footwear. He looked good, fit, business-
like.

Always a hard worker, his eyes scanned past the yellow
crime scene tape, a narrow strip of plastic printed repeatedly with the words POLICE LINE DO NOT CROSS. What
the detective saw startled him. What he saw riveted his
entire visual range to one spot.

There, beneath the American flag, sat his best friend,
Sam Walker. Reaching Sam in an instant, Ridge noted his
friend's solemn, haggard face. Blood stained his clothes,
grime tainted his skin, shock staked a claim on his face.

"Where is your family?" Ridge asked, referring to Sam's
wife, Bailey, and their daughters, Fern and Sage. He silently prayed they were safe.

A flicker of relief breezed across Sam's face when he saw
his friend. "Home."

Concern rumbled its way inside Ridge's professional mind. He asked gently, "Did you call Bailey?"

Sam's voice was hoarse, subdued, completely different from Ridge's private experience of it. "Yeah, I didn't wanna have her worry about how late I'm getting home. She's waiting for me now."

The sound of crickets loud in his ear, Ridge asked softly, "What happened?"

Sam was tired, his deep voice hollow, though his spirit lifted in his friend's welcome company. He turned his eyes away from the corpse that lay on the ground nearby. "I worked late tonight. On the way home, I stopped to buy iced tea for me and Bailey. When I left the store to get in my car, five skinheads followed a lone kid to this parking lot just to beat him to death. The world is crazy, Ridge."

Sam turned his gaze upon the detective, his eyes on fire with his need to avenge the young victim's life. His throat ached to scream his frustration, his rage at the tragic outcome of the deadly brawl.

Straightforward and exact, Ridge took a memo pad from the inner breast pocket of his light-weight suit jacket. From the same breast pocket he removed a silver mechanical pencil, the pencil he used to copy his special brand of shorthand.

He said, "Since the assailants pushed you away instead of beating you, I think the boy was targeted."

Sam frowned, only dimly aware of the gentle rise and fall of hushed background conversation, a sound he suspected was normal for this type of event. Sobs filtered to him through the steady thrum of human voices. His own tears were long gone. "But why?"

Ridge watched Carlyle supervise the collection of physical evidence. "I don't know, but I intend to find out. Can you describe the gang members?"

"The blonde girl wore a black T-shirt with the Confederate flag stitched across the back, camouflage pants, and military boots. She was thin; skinny face, stick arms, little legs. She was probably five-feet-six."

Ridge flipped his six-by-four-inch memo pad to a fresh, crisp page. "What about the other girl?"

"I pegged her at five-feet flat, 110 pounds, a brunette."

"Clothes?"

"Military boots, black T-shirt with FIGHT ZOG on the back, regular straight-leg jeans."

"And the others?"

"Three males," Sam answered gravely, running a hand across the short waves of his hair, hair that faded to nothing at the nape. "Late teens or early twenties. I have names plus descriptions, only I don't know which names match the bodies."

Ridge peered into Sam's eyes. "I'll match them. Describe what you remember, starting with the names."

"Bash, Snake, Grip."

Ridge was puzzled, unfamiliar with the code names, anxious to get to the police station in order to research the computer files for viable connections. "Go on."

"Punk One was the leader," Sam recalled, his bushy brows drawn tightly together. "The boy's head was shaved with ragged bangs chopped off at eye level. Like the blonde, he wore a black T-shirt with a Confederate flag on the back, camouflage pants and military boots. He used a wooden baseball bat."

"What about Punk Two?"

Sam shifted his six-foot body into a more comfortable position. "Punk Two's head was bald with a swastika tattooed on the right side. He wore a black T-shirt without symbols, camouflage pants and military boots. He used an aluminum bat."

"And the last?"

Still charged by the tragedy, Sam's memory was sharp, concise, vivid. "Punk Three had a badly pitted face. His hair was buzzed short. He wore an olive green undershirt,

camouflage pants and military boots with metal toes. His
arms were heavily tattooed."

"Do you remember the patterns?"

"On the left arm were the words WHITE POWER. On
the right arm was the American flag."

"Did the victim say anything critical to the case?" Ridge
queried, watching two male officials lift the victim's body
from the gritty ground onto a collapsible metal gurney,
and roll the gurney to a waiting emergency vehicle. The
coroner herself had come and gone, after an initial exami-
nation.

"No." The response was brutal with intensity.

Sam watched Ridge flip his memo pad closed, retract
the lead in his mechanical pencil, slip the pad and the
pencil inside his breast pocket, and pause to listen. Nervous laughter rang from a small group of people, spectators
who found excitement in the night's unexpected drama.

Sam was alert to everything around him. His nose picked
up the scent of a freshly lit match, a telling prelude to the
pungent odor of smoking tobacco. In his experience,
smokers lit up as much to manage anxiety as they did for
pleasure; the look on the smoker's craggy face revealed
both.

Sam was a man who could scarcely contain his rage.
Looking at him, Ridge felt far from professional. He was
a friend who shared the pain of someone he cared about
in his private life. Sentiment clashed with duty as he said,
"I promise you, Sam, I'll catch them."

The best friends shook hands. Their grasp turned into
a brotherly hug, a hug as truly solemn and real to the men
as the gleaming gray wagon that carried the victim's body
to the city morgue.

Three

Wearing cut-offs and a red cropped top, Bailey flung herself into her husband's arms as he walked through their living room door. He was filthy, tired, and grateful to see the love smoldering deep within her pretty brown eyes. It was 11:00 P.M.

"I've been shaking ever since you called from the store," she admitted, her anxious gaze searching his face, questioning his health after the fight. This was the second time in their marriage they had faced a murder.

"I'm okay," he replied to her silent question, his body welcoming the sweet feel of her palms against the hard bones of his shoulders, the tough length of his arms, the muscled width of his waist. His strain was a tangible thing, a thing she felt inside and out.

"I couldn't believe what you were telling me." Her wandering gaze lit on the slightly rough, familiar skin of his face, bruised from the fight. It had begun to swell a little. "I'm so glad you're okay."

"I still can't believe it, and I was there," he murmured against the top of her head. The rose scent of her hair wafted through his nose. In the midst of his great anger over the gang beating, his senses relished the familiar fragrance. He savored her comfort. He savored her.

He led her to their living room, a cozy room scattered with gleaming brass lamps. They sat together in the center of their sofa, each thankful for the moment and for the other. Sam assessed the problem they faced, his terrible anger, and the best way to deal with it.

"I was so mad I could hardly see straight," he continued. "Everything happened so fast. In ten minutes, those punks were gone."

Her chagrin was visible at his last remark. Her fingers squeezed his wrist. "Tell me what happened." Race violence, an issue often relegated to private conversation, was now in the open. She understood his hostility. The kid who died might have been one of their daughters.

After Sam told her what happened, Bailey laid a hand on the taut flesh of his thigh in a desire to soothe him, to show him they suffered together, not alone. He was too strong to want her to mother him, too proud to say he hurt like hell in body and in spirit. She respected his control in a volatile situation. She decided to match his strength with more of her own.

"You saw the boy running from the Thunderbird to the convenience store," she restated, her tone and face thoughtful. "I bet he lives in the neighborhood because he was on foot. Did he look familiar to you?"

"No, but the car they drove did look familiar," Sam recalled, his voice gruff. "I was thinking about the car on the ride home from the store. I've got a hunch I've seen it. I just can't think where or when."

The way he nibbled his lower lip showed Bailey the depth of his worry; the nervous habit was one she had learned to recognize over the years. "Did you get the license plate tags?" she asked, linking his hands with her own.

Sam liked the soft feel of her fingers, the healing comfort in them. Drawing the energy from her strength, he blew a long breath, a harsh breath that slammed against the small space between them.

"Missing."

The word "premeditation" stepped into Bailey's mind. Her curiosity aroused, she tapped an index finger against her bottom lip. "Since the tags were missing, I bet the attack was planned."

"Ridge thinks so too."

Bailey sat up straighter. "Ridge is on the case?"

"Yeah, he and Carlyle Higgins."

Ridge had helped the Walkers solve their first murder case, a case that happened before Sage was born. They knew Carlyle as a friend and Ridge's co-worker. "Did you tell them what you saw?"

"Ridge interviewed me briefly tonight. Tomorrow we're gonna try it again after he sorts through the evidence the police find in the parking lot."

His pause was short. "I keep wondering if the people in that Thunderbird wanted to kill that kid, or if they just wanted to beat him up for fun. I wonder if he was chosen at random."

Bailey's voice turned husky. "Either thought is chilling."

"Real life is more scary than fiction, Bailey, more scary than the news on TV. Seeing somebody beat to death has gotta be the biggest sin on the planet. I'm gonna make sure those creeps make it to jail."

All Bailey's heart, all her love, all her hope converged into two simple words, "Oh, Sam."

Rising swiftly, he paced away from her, his voice brazen with grief, his body pumped with hatred, feelings he expressed as anger. He slammed his fist against the wall, hard. "I've got blood on my hands, Bailey, and I didn't kill anybody. I didn't kill anybody, but for a minute I wanted to."

Bailey made herself stay seated, keenly aware Sam craved a brutal revenge that ran against the law, that ran so deep inside him it struck the primitive man. He whirled to face her. "I'm so mad I'm crazy with it. I'm gonna find them, Bailey. I'm gonna make sure they get what they deserve."

Bailey felt ferocious, like a lioness ready to defend, ready

o protect her family. With all her heart she wanted to
erase the anguish he felt, but knew it was pain he had to
work through on his own. She wanted him to know she
was on his side. "What shall we do?"

"Get a gun and kick ass with it." Bailey knew he was
angry so she let him vent without interrupting. Neither of
them believed private citizens should own guns, especially
with children in the house.

"The murdering punks, Bailey. I hate what they did!"

"Me, too."

Sam's rage was a deadly force in their living room. "I'm
buying a gun."

"No."

She knew it was the anger talking, knew he spoke this
way because he trusted her with the deepest, darkest feelings he ever felt in his life. She was his reason and conscience in rough situations. He had done the same thing
for her during their first murder mystery.

"Yes," he argued.

"A gun brings with it a different set of problems. Your
parents will watch the girls while we look for the skinheads'
car. You said it looked familiar. It's got to be around here
somewhere. Why don't we look?"

"Say we find the car, then what?" he challenged. "We
gotta use a gun to hang on to them until the police get a
hold of them." A raw wave of anger washed over Sam. It
was sharp, penetrating, ominous. "I can't stand around
doing nothing. Those skinheads have gotta pay."

Bailey debated arguing with him, then decided to go for
it because it had never been their policy to let conflict
build into a crisis within their relationship. "I'm not asking
you to stand around. I'm asking you to think, just like you
got me to think through our first mystery. If you go after
those skinheads with a weapon tonight, it may be you going
to jail tomorrow instead of them. I don't want to lose you.
I couldn't take it."

It seemed an infinity before he spoke again. His face was hard and ruthless. "Before the boy died he told me thank you. Can you believe that? Thank you."

Bailey stood up from the sofa and slipped her arms around his waist. The scowl on his face did not intimidate her because she knew he loved her and the life they had built together. She knew he was hurting and reacting to that pain.

She squeezed him tight as if she would never let him go, using her body to express the comfort she longed to give. "My whole body hurts just hearing about what happened. I feel bad for him and his family. How old was he?"

"He looked to be around fifteen or sixteen."

"A baby," she murmured, wanting comfort where no comfort could be found.

Sam wiped away the tears that traced the curve of her cheeks. "The kid was brave, more brave than some men twice his age. He stood up to his attackers even though he carried no weapon and was outnumbered. The strangest thing of all is that when he died, he smiled."

"Smiled?"

"Yeah," Sam confirmed, troubled by the fleeting image. "He lay in my arms, struggling to open his eyes and trying to speak and yet accepting his death without fear. Good God, he was brave!"

"That's beautiful."

"Yeah." They held each other for a long time. "Stand by me, Bailey. That's all I ask."

She covered his palm with both of her own shaky ones. "Always."

Sam glared into space, his thoughts heavy with the recent past and the troubled future. In minutes his world had been turned upside down. "That kid won't get up tomorrow, but I will. It's a creepy feeling."

She softened, knowing such an admission was costly to a proud man. She loved him all the more for trusting her with his naked feelings. "Even though the boy suffered, he didn't die alone. Maybe that's why he smiled. He had you, a strong man who kept his body from resting against a dirty sidewalk during his last few moments in this world. That means something."

Sam ran a large hand over his head, the waves of his hair coarse against his skin. Being melancholy would not change what happened. He did not want to feel soft and forgiving. He wanted justice and revenge for a crime that was wrong no matter how he looked at it.

"This didn't have to happen!" he raged.

Bailey sought to heal, sought to give him some of the great store of her personal strength. This was the man she adored and she wanted to help him. "You care because you're a good, kind, giving man. I love your strength. I love you."

Taking in her words, taking in the energy from her strength, he stared once more into space, his thick brows pushed together in deep thought. "When I stood beside him to fight, I felt like a soldier, not a father or a husband. I couldn't believe what was happening."

"It was as if I watched it all from a distance. I'll never be the same man again, Bailey, never."

The idea singed his comfort zone, redefined his natural self into a new, scarred, formidable entity. He was a conquerer, a champion, a hero. The battle was not over, it had just begun.

Harnessing her love for Sam in the stronghold of her arms, Bailey squeezed him with all her might. That night, in ten minutes his world had become a living hell of intense emotion. "I feel your pain and I don't know how to help you. Not knowing how to help you is a terrible thing."

His smoldering black gaze rolled all over her five-feet-five inches. The red top she wore brought out the fine color of her skin. The cut-off jeans she wore showcased her lean, sturdy thighs.

She was warmth, sincerity, hearth, home. She was his woman, now and forever. "You're being here is enough."

She touched a finger to the grime on his shirt, the move reminding her of how much worse things could have been that night, how narrow his escape had been from death or serious injury. Her blessings, in that moment, were many.

"What do you know about skinheads?" she asked.

Tiny lines of stress sketched the corners of Sam's eyes. "They've probably got a connection with the Ku Klux Klan, people we already know use bully tactics and violence to get what they want."

Chills gripped Bailey as she considered the complex nature of hate groups and the people who run them. She thought about the skinheads, wondering why they chose New Hope to wreak havoc. "Vigilantes."

"Yeah."

"I don't get it."

"Tonight, right now, I understand that wild, sort of . . . insane urge," Sam admitted, the words sounding harsh, unyielding, totally unlike his usual even-keeled self. "Part of me wants to arm myself and go out to track the skinheads down. I want them strung up, Bailey, not put in jail."

"I understand how you could feel that way."

"Right now I envy Ridge his bullets and his badge," Sam confessed, the deep grooves in his cheeks pronounced by the weight of his conscience. This was not a statement of defeat, it was a statement of fact.

Armed, with the law behind him, he could make sure the skinheads were brought to justice in a legal way, Ridge's way. Without bullets and a badge he would have to bring the skinheads down another way, his way.

Sam cut his eyes over to Bailey, the expression in them as glossy as a child's marble, only this was no game they played. This was real life, real drama, real pain. "I bet that boy's family won't be upset if I get rid of the people who killed their son."

"I doubt it."

His body was taut, packed with coiled tendon over hard, dense bone. His brows were as thick as the frightening ideas of revenge that lay behind them. He felt caged by the law. All he wanted to do was arm himself for a battle that no one man alone could win. He solved this problem by narrowing the battle down to one man and his woman against a gang of five people. Bailey was his right arm and confidant.

She listened as he released more anger, a healthy thing because it helped them understand exactly what they were dealing with together. "I want blood for blood. I don't want to say, *Let the police handle it,* or *What happened was meant to be,* or *I guess it was his time to die.* I don't wanna be moderate or reasonable. I wanna knock heads."

Mixed feelings stormed through Bailey as his emotion moved her to say, "I love you."

Her eyes were wet, round pools of sincerity. Her love was all she had to give in that moment. She could not control what he said or did in his life, she could only share that life as his lover and mate. With her heart, mind, body, and soul she belonged to him.

Her devotion swept over him from bottom to top. "It's your love that's keeping me grounded right now," he confessed. His face was inches from her face, his breath mingling with her breath. "I don't have words to say exactly what I'm feeling. I don't understand it all myself. I've never wanted to," the pause was deafening, "hurt anybody before."

Bailey grasped for a lifeline, an alternative to her love because her love was only a part of the medicine he needed. He needed a man's understanding, a man's common ground, a man's view of a world that turned tragic when least expected, like a stop at a convenience store on the way home to buy iced tea. He also needed action.

"Maybe talking to Ridge will help," she suggested. "He's trained to handle violent crime."

Sam studied Bailey, all the while thinking that what he felt for the skinheads tainted the love he felt for his wife. By carrying those destructive feelings inside of him, he brought something ugly into his beautiful home. He planned to change those feelings, soon.

He said, "They can't go free."

Bailey ran a hand through her straight, shoulder-length hair. "I agree. I'm stressed out about what happened tonight, too. Violence strips away polite ways. It makes people scared. I'm scared."

"I'll protect you."

Bailey leaned her calves against the coffee table top, her ankles crossed. Her shoulder felt good next to his shoulder. "I know. It's just that when people tell me slavery is over and I should forget about it, I tell those people my great-grandmother was the daughter of a slave. That's my history, I tell them.

"It's ugly, it's real, but it's mine. That history is the basis for the racism you confronted tonight. It scares me to think times haven't changed, they are just different. Tonight racism was an excuse for violence."

"My parents taught me to pick my battles," Sam said. "I tell Fern and Sage the same thing. That's what I'm doing now, picking my battle. A man's gotta stand up to crime in his own neighborhood. What happened tonight was wrong, and I won't rest until justice is served."

"I'm with you."

"That's good because I'm gonna find those skinheads and when I find those punks, I'm gonna kick ass."

Bailey knew he wanted more, much more. She pressed her lips together, her practical mind running along the same lines as Sam's. They needed a plan, but it had to be his plan, a plan based on what he saw, what he felt, since the gang beating was witnessed and felt by him.

It had been the same when they faced their first murder mystery, only their roles had been reversed. This time the drama centered on Sam. She believed it was her role to meet him halfway and to work with him one hundred percent. It was her turn to play Watson to his Sherlock.

One of the many things she admired about him was his ability to take charge. He was an old-fashioned, down to earth, commanding man. It invigorated her to watch him pit his strength and wits against the band of villains. She knew that even without bullets and a badge Sam was a force to be reckoned with, and she matched him stride for stride with practical thinking skills.

This ability to think along the same lines was the benefit of living closely together for so many years, a benefit that helped them to understand each other completely. What they understood but did not fully discuss was Sam's underlying fear. To express his fear would be a sign of weakness when he needed so much to feel strong. It was Bailey who voiced this fear, a fear he was too proud to express because acknowledging the fear would diminish his anger. He needed the anger to fuel his quest for clues.

She spoke for them both. "What happened tonight can happen anywhere at anytime. The random feel of it is frightening."

He stroked her palms with his thumbs. His touch was gentle despite the harsh stillness in his manner. "That's why I gotta do something to stop it from happening again around here. We go to that store at least twice a week between the two of us—me to buy lottery tickets, you to buy the Sunday paper. Everything about that store seemed so normal and safe."

"I'm proud of the way you stood up for that boy tonight," she admitted. Even though they had covered this subject once before, it was without the quiet that lay between them now. She needed to talk as much as he needed to act.

Sam threw his head back so that he gazed at the molding along the rim of the ceiling. After a few seconds, he closed his eyes. "I've never felt such rage, Bailey," he said, more to himself than to her.

"It's okay to let go," she offered, believing that everything in life happened for a good reason, even if that reason was not obvious to those people looking for answers to questions about the mysteries of life. A plaque hung on the wall in their kitchen that read: *Life is a mystery to be lived, not a problem to be solved.* She believed this too.

Sam stared down at her, loving every little thing he saw. Living with Bailey, a spiritual woman, only strengthened *his* earthy mentality. Because of her, he lived his greatest fantasy: to be loved deeply by a beautiful woman, to return that love in full measure.

In the solace of their living room, he appreciated having joined himself with her in marriage. This act was one of the best decisions he had ever made in his adult life. Aside from being an attentive wife and caring mother, she shared their happiness through the food she cooked, food that usually fit every occasion in their lives.

Bailey's meals nursed well-being inside guests at their dinner table. For Sam, the well-being was sprinkled like salt or pepper right along with the three main spices in their married life: truth, beauty, and goodness.

He studied her lovely face as if he might never see it again. What he saw in her was precious and good. She was the light on the other side of a terrible experience. "Everything that counts most in a person is strong in you, Bailey."

"Oh, Sam."

He shook his head, aware his introspection ran deeper this night than usual. He was not normally this spiritual, but after the boy's murder he felt the need to honor his blessings with conscious thought.

He stood, drawing Bailey up with him, her size-seven body firm and curvaceous beside his. "Let's check on the girls."

The couple went first into twelve-year-old Fern's dainty bedroom, a spacious room with a lovely menagerie of unique ornaments, each with special meaning for their owner. A collection of music boxes stood on mated bedside tables.

Built-in book shelves lined one wall, while a profusion of bold florals and stripes dominated the bedding. The window treatments, in primary shades of yellow, blue, and green were made of the same sturdy fabric as the bedding.

A quilt in an around-the-world pattern lay crumpled at the foot of the twin bed where Fern slept. A tall, thin girl, she was ebony-hued like her father. Her hair of heavy braids lay free upon her feather-stuffed pillow. Reverently, Sam angled his body toward hers so that his kiss against her cheek was gentle.

In Sage's bedroom, he smiled indulgently at the complete disarray. While Fern's bookshelves were lined with books, four-year-old Sage's shelves were filled with toys. The pine-framed bed was stained peach. Hand painted flowers decorated the head and foot boards. Fruit prints dominated the large room in shades of violet, red, and green.

Sage slept with an arm dangling from the bed. Warm feelings running through him, Sam settled her arm to rest beneath the pink cotton sheet. Satin ribbons fell away from hair that billowed against her feather filled pillow. Her skin was cocoa-colored and baby soft. He grazed her nose with a soft kiss.

Knowing his daughters were safe invigorated him, their well-being the very heart of his emotional recovery. He thought he would lose his mind if what happened to the dead teen happened to one of his children.

"Did the girls give you a whole lotta trouble when they went to bed tonight?" he asked, wanting to discuss something normal, wanting to make his world right again. Bed-time rituals were familiar.

Bailey laughed a little, in tune with his train of thought. "For a change, no. They claimed they were too tired to take a bath, but I made them take one anyway. You should've seen the dirt on Sage's face."

He smiled at the image. Their youngest child's face was often smudged with food. She loved to snack, and whatever she ate tended to be messy, especially on a day like today, spent in an amusement park. She never left the park without eating at least one hot dog and a spool of cotton candy.

"I can imagine."

Bailey heard the hint of laughter in his voice and rejoiced at the beautiful sound. It enveloped her with marvelous, inexplicable sensation. Everything was going to be alright. "I'm glad you're home."

He caressed the soft, warm nape of her hair. "So am I."

In the master suite, she donned a pale lavender cotton gown that stopped just above the knees as she waited for him to emerge from their glass encased shower. She sat at her vanity bench, a firm rectangular bench covered in tapestry fabric.

Her thoughts disquieted, she lifted a bottle of scent from the vanity. The label affixed to it read *Lauren*. It was Sam's favorite perfume, a fresh, floral scent she wore as a silent gift between lovers, a gift that pleased them both.

She sprayed it carefully, paying special attention to the backs of her knees, the pulse points between her thighs, the hollow between her breasts. The pretty scent clung to the crook of her elbows; favorite haunts of Sam's. Last, she touched the fragrance against the line of smooth flesh behind each of her ears.

Deep in thought about what Sam had witnessed, she used her fingers to comb the red-brown length of her straightened hair, wiry strands she rinsed with rosewater once a week, something she also did for the girls as a treat.

Using the tip of an index finger, she fanned the lashes that framed her wide, deep ochre-colored eyes. The gesture brought order to lashes that were lush and glossy in texture. Flicking her tongue against the small pad of her right pinkie, she smoothed its moist tip against her brows, a graceful move that eased them into place.

Ready for him to join her, she surveyed their bedroom. Candles were scattered about the sumptuous suite. She preferred not to use them this night, in deference to the brutal experience still fresh in Sam's mind.

Instead of candle fire, she illuminated the bedroom with three-way lamps set on the second switch. The emerald-colored ceramic lamps stood on tables at either side of the king size, cherry wood canopied bed. Family photographs, framed in silver, adorned the bedside tables along with a simmering bowl of sandalwood potpourri.

In the shower, water rolled off Sam in steaming beads, liquid pools that gained momentum the farther down his body they traveled; over his face, across his neck, down his shoulder blades, over his back, across his rump, down his thighs to his calves and feet. The water's cleansing trek eased his lingering temper, though not completely.

As the muscles in his body uncoiled, Sam's mind flexed with purpose, a resolve to do something positive in the neighborhood which could counterbalance the attack against the young man. His death now tainted the lives of his murderers. This truth baffled Sam.

What motivated tonight's gang? he questioned. Greed? Why did they come to New Hope? To make a statement? Was New Hope targeted for racist crime because its citizens were mostly people of color? Solemn, Sam wondered if he would find answers to the questions that troubled him.

In the bedroom, Bailey worried about how close the teen's death hit home, so close to her own backyard she felt sick. She was certain the skinhead beating was no accident because they were not a normal part of the neighborhood. If they were, she might suspect a gang rivalry, one that had resulted in death. This was not the case.

Finding events that preceded Sam's coming home to her confusing, Bailey listened as he turned off the long running shower. Attentive, she heard its glass door slide open, then close.

As she imagined him dressing, she knew his mind spun toward possibilities, constructive ways to deal with the tragedy he had seen by chance or by design. When it got down to it, she believed all things in life were connected, and that all events happened for a specific reason.

She wished she could change time and circumstance in order to erase the savage event. Because this was not possible, she resolved to heal Sam's body and spirit in the best way she knew how, through deep love and physical closeness.

The click of the bathroom door signaled his arrival, an entrance Bailey watched with a gleam in her eye. His muscles stretched like thunder in motion, with a leashed power that never failed to excite her. Her carousing gaze straddled every inch of his rough-haired body.

Dressed for bed, the man she loved faced her, his warm arms stretching the short gap between them. His fingers were caught firmly within the silken web of her own. Their wedding rings reflected the mellow glow of the lamps.

She squeezed his strong, rough hands. Even in the midst of their sadness, she loved the way he felt whenever they touched, whenever they were alone in the sanctity of their bedroom. He took her in his arms.

She shivered with stirring pleasure as he wrapped a lock of her hair around the calloused tip of his left index finger. Lowering his head, he lifted the lock to his nose and inhaled the alluring scent of rosewater. The scent charmed him.

With the same finger he traced the smooth length of her jaw. He began at the outer corner of her right eye and progressed to the left. His motions deft, he pulled her closer into the intimate circle of his arms. She felt like she was every good thing he ever wanted, every sweet dream he ever knew.

In turn she savored his strength. The dense bulk of his body contoured hers so completely that she fit his form in all the right places. She noticed the comforting beat of his heart as it thumped against her cheek. The spot was familiar. The spot was just right.

She felt his breath whisper warm and soft against her brow. The iron pressure of his thighs grazed against the firmness of hers, a touch that spiraled a thread of desire through her loving spirit.

New Hope, the wonderful town where they lived, and its troubles with skinheads, was briefly forgotten as the dark dream of his body drew her into a special heaven, a heaven free of death and pain, a heaven peopled only by the two of them.

In this secret place, the human song of their kindred spirits enveloped them, soothing their sentient souls. The middle-eastern scent of burning sandalwood stole into each lover's breath, its therapeutic aroma renewing the couple in beauty and in health. His mouth anchored gently on her lips in a stimulating kiss.

The bracing kiss spurred them into an extraordinary, united state of mind. On a subconscious level they shared a powerful union centered on nurturing and commitment. The devotion they knew was so profound they kindled, stoked, and savored it until the fragrant island of their bedroom became the only world that ever was or would be.

Bailey swayed against her gentleman lover as, like a bandit, he stole her breath away. Like a sculptor, he kneaded the warm clay of her love; like a soldier, he slayed the dragons that stood between them, one by one.

Four

Meanwhile in Trinity City the leader of the skinhead gang played back the recent hours in his mind. A former philosophy student and current bookworm, Snake enjoyed every opportunity to show off his thinking skills. "Remember this guys, we live in a war. In wars, people die."

"Yeah," Bash agreed, "Tonight we jumped that guy as a unit. We stand together."

Grip glared at his friends. "We left evidence."

Agitated, Digits lifted the television's remote control from a scarred coffee table, littered with cigarette butts and beer cans. She flipped off the twenty-five-inch television set, its fake wood exterior covered in gray dust. "Things got out of hand tonight."

Snake negated the idea. "You realized tonight that you have the strength not simply to kill, but to watch someone be killed. Nothing got out of hand because we did what we set out to do, which was to have a little boot party."

Snake spoke with cool authority. Through reading, he had learned how to create his own subculture, a culture influenced by other organized supremacist societies: Christian Identity, the John Birch Society, James Warner's New Christian Crusade, White Aryan Resistance, and the Ku Klux Klan. This knowledge helped him create his gang, Satan's Magic.

For Snake, life was a survival game for the fittest. "Tomorrow night I'm meeting two new guys to recruit."

Bash cocked his head to the side. "Why?"

"They know weapons," Snake answered. "The boot party tonight was our initiation into the battlefield of race war."

Grip pressed his palms against either side of his face. "This is wrong, man. It's not a game anymore."

"It was never a game," Snake admonished. "I chose each of you for a specific reason. I chose Bash for his reckless, forceful mind. I chose Grip for his natural ability to cover everybody's back. Holiday walks easily between the left-wing world and the right. Digits questions everything, which makes me think even harder. All of you make up a solid core group of people I can trust."

Digits forced long, slow breaths through her open mouth. "Yeah, but—"

"You didn't do one thing you didn't want to do," Snake interrupted.

Bash looked at her. "You need a good thrashing in the bedroom. It'll ease your tension. Mine, too."

Digits sniffed in disdain. "I won't sleep with you."

Bash was calm. "We both know you want to do it as much as I do, Digits." Like the other men, Bash was slightly battered and more than a little dirty from the fight, but that did not stop him from being horny.

"She's a hellion," Snake chortled, enjoying Bash's struggle to conquer, his struggle to prove himself a man in front of his leader. Snake knew how much Bash wanted to be second in command of Satan's Magic. He let him work for it.

Digits threw her beer can against the poster of Hitler's face that hung against the wall. The tin can hit its target where it clattered, then hit the carpeted floor with a soft thud. She watched the can rock from side to side, then

stop, a small trickle of liquid dripping from the hole in its
top. She jammed her fingers through her tangled hair.

Excited by her rush of temper, Bash licked his narrow
lips. Every heightened sensation of the night converged
on the lower limbs of his body. He needed a release. He
needed sex.

"Come here, girl," he beckoned her.

Though her future was vague, Digits knew what came
next between herself and Bash. "No."

He squinted, nearly laughing at her refusal. They both
knew sex was always good between them, especially when
their emotions ran high. "No?"

She tossed her head. "You heard me."

He thrilled to her challenge the same way he relished the
role of conqueror. Hyped on murder, high on crank, he felt
numb to the consequences of his greedy, self-centered needs.
He was horny as he ever was when it came to getting Digits
between the wrinkled cotton sheets on Snake's bed.

"What I heard was a challenge," he firmly stated. All he
saw was the stiffness in her body, a stiffness he aimed to
melt down with lust. His groin readied for the action.

Grip leaned forward, his hands clasped hard between
his knees. "Leave her alone."

Bash turned on him, fire in his eyes. "You ain't got nothing to say about it."

Snake looked at them all, then picked up the remote
control for the television set. He flipped through the channels, then adjusted the sound. He looked at the fighting
couple. "Settle your business."

Bash boldly stated his objective. "Girl, I'm gonna make
you holler."

Digits felt the beginnings of intense desire. She never
shared a bed with Bash without making him work for it.
She tossed him another verbal obstacle. "You have no business ordering me around."

Bash eyed her small breasts. "None."

The mere thought of her wrapped in his tough, strong arms atop Snake's double sized mattress caused Bash to shiver in salacious, greedy delight. Digits saw his sensual shiver and shivered herself.

From experience, every person in Snake's apartment knew what came next between the battling couple. Bash would slap her face, then Digits would slap him back. The wooden headboard in the back bedroom would slam against the wall a dozen times, then more.

He crossed the room to face her. "Come here," he crooned. "Let's not argue all night."

Digits narrowed her eyes at him. Her throat twitched as she studied the man whose rough brand of sex repeatedly claimed her despite the captivated audience, despite her token resistance, despite her dislike of the small back bedroom, its only window opened wide to a red brick wall. She turned away from him.

Bash moved toward her with the lithe ease of a gymnast. When he reached Digits, he tossed her struggling body over his shoulder. Not in the least disturbed, she pounded his back with her fists. Bash held on to few disciplines except for his lean, fit body. He kept his head clean-shaven so that the swastika tattooed on the right side of it was always visible.

His conquering attitude excited Snake who watched him with avid interest. Once the bedroom door slammed shut he heard Bash slap Digits, then he heard Digits slapping him back. Their rough mating ritual had begun.

Grip glared at the television screen. He tried to block the sex sounds that escaped through the crack beneath the bedroom door. He knew it would remain closed for some time to come, a thought that sickened him. His scowl deepened.

His badly pitted face made it possible for him to look menacing without trying too hard to get the job done. His buzzed haircut supported his brutal appearance. This image caused some people to cross the street when he walked their way. This made him feel special.

For him, image was everything, but mostly it was power. Grip refused to wear a black T-shirt like the others. His muscular arms were heavily tattooed with the boldly printed words HITLER, PURE, WAR. On his left arm were the words WHITE POWER. On the right arm was the American flag.

None of the symbols meant a thing to him just then. Just then he cared nothing about the volatile words he carried everywhere on his body. He cared nothing about what happened at Jasper Mini Mart that night. He failed to care because in the next room a headboard slammed with increasing rhythm against a blank wall; bam, bam, bam.

With his hands, Grip squeezed his knees at the sound, squeezed his knees until the skin on his knuckles stretched thin across the bones. The three words, *let her be*, rang in his troubled mind, but he had never said those three words. He had never staked his claim to the only woman he had ever loved.

Saturday

Backstairs Influence

Five

"I like it when you wash my hair, Daddy," Sage said once Sam had wrapped her head in a large pink towel, turban style. It was 8:00 A.M.

"You and me both, pumpkin," he replied as he planted a kiss on her soft cheek. She felt small and delicate in his arms, though she was plump all over.

"Is that how come you wash us girls' hair on Hair Day?" she asked as she played with a strand of red brown hair, hair the same shade as her mother's. She already knew the answer to the question. Sam knew that she repeated the same questions to reinforce the positive in her life, even though it sometimes drove him crazy.

As he met her eyes in the mirror before them, he saw the way her dark gaze adored him. It showed him that she bet her daddy could do anything he set his mind to doing because he was so tall and strong. Feeling cherished, Sam's chest swelled with pride.

"Yep," he replied, grinning at her before tucking a loose strand of wet hair beneath her towel. If ever he needed to lighten his mood, Sage was the ticket.

She talked so much while he washed her hair he had little time to think about the troubles he had found at the convenience store Friday night. She demanded his full attention, something he never minded giving because it made him feel useful.

Dressed in yellow shorts and a matching cotton top,

Sage's eyes sparkled with mischief. "You 'specially like washing Mommy's hair, huh?" she asked, her tone coy as she fished for compliments from the greatest man in the world.

"All three of you." He laughed when she fluttered her lashes.

If he said that he only liked doing Bailey's hair he would disappoint Sage and Fern. Aware the day was a blessing, Sam thanked God for allowing him to share it with the people he cared most about in the world, his wife and daughters.

"But you make Mommy giggle," Sage pointed out as if testing her father's devotion to her, as if making sure his love was as strong for her as it was for her pretty mother and sister. "You and Mommy always play together."

Rinsing hair conditioner from the sink, Sam chuckled at his youngest child's outspoken behavior. She seldom bit her tongue when it came to speaking her mind, a habit he and Bailey guided rather than squelched altogether, which they thought might stifle her creative spirit. Instead, they enjoyed her opinions, often considering them objective and accurate rather than cruel or sarcastic. Sage was smart.

"Oh yeah?" he teased her, enjoying the way she admired him with her winning smile and trust. He felt larger than life just then.

"Unh huh," she assured him, her manner matter of fact, her dimpled fingers on hips made stout by her mother's cooking. "Every time you kiss Mommy on the neck when her head's unner water she giggles."

Sage explained her position in a self assured tone that showed her dad she had given the subject a lot of thought. Her conversation reminded him she truly was no longer a baby, even though he saw her as one. At nearly five, she would be ready for kindergarten soon.

"Don't I make you giggle, too?" he said.

Sage batted her lashes. "Yeah," she answered flirtatiously, like a seasoned coquette.

"Like this?" he asked. He tickled her belly until she toppled off her tole painted footstool into his arms, shrieking with laughter.

Pulling her close to rest against him, Sam shut his eyes, his senses swirling with wonder at how good, at how warm Sage felt to him, how reassuringly alive. Rocking softly to the rhythm of strong emotions that enveloped him completely, he remembered the dead young man, once as small and trusting in his father's arms as Sage was for him just now. Ripped through with despair, he squeezed her with a gruff tenderness.

She grinned, oblivious to her father's secret conflicts. He treated her the same way he always did, with tender affection. "Yeah," she squealed, "like that!"

Sam blow dried her hair, now scented with her mother's rosewater. "We're done," he replied, "let's find Mommy."

In the den, Bailey worked on the last two cornrows she used to decorate Fern's head for the girls' weekend at Sam's parents' house. The cornrows were an easy way to keep Fern's coarse hair in pretty condition without a lot of fuss.

To style Fern's hair in cornrows Bailey combed the wiry tresses into a loose ponytail at the top center of her head. Gathering a small amount of hair with the forefingers of each hand, she formed one narrow row after another by weaving strands from the scalp with strands from the top layer of hair.

The work was slow and methodical, a meditation for Bailey as she considered Sam's problem, considered how to help him. Her mind was split between the domestic chore of tending her daughter and the problem of tending her husband's anger and grief. Bailey focused on her handiwork.

The cornrows ran from Fern's forehead to her crown, not stopping until the ends of Fern's hair were reached.

At each end Bailey secured the braid with a lavender butterfly clip.

After all the sections were even, she angled them toward the crown of Fern's head. The plastic butterfly clip was removed then the braids were twisted into a topknot. Bailey secured the topknots with bobby pins sliding the final bobby pin in place just as Sam entered the sunroom with Sage in his arms. She was nearly finished.

"Perfect timing," she complimented him, thinking he looked great in olive shorts with the name of his company, New Generation, printed on his T-shirt. She never tired of the sight of Sam holding one or the other of their daughters in his arms.

When he came home from work, he would stretch his strong arms out wide, legs akimbo for support so that the girls could hang off either sturdy bicep, their legs dangling above the floor as they shrieked their pleasure at his performance.

In truth, Sam and Bailey knew Fern was growing too old for this father-daughter routine, but they understood that seeing Sage hanging from her daddy's arm kept babyhood feelings close for Fern; after all, her father was her hero too.

Sam surveyed Bailey's crafting skills. "Aren't you tired?" he asked, aware she had been at it for more than an hour.

Fern sat on a cushion on the floor between her mother's knees. Saturday morning cartoons animated the television while hair products were scattered on the coffee table within easy reach of Bailey's experienced hands. Sam enjoyed the wholesome scene. It made him thankful he lived an ordinary, healthy life when he was not faced with a murder mystery.

"A little," she admitted, her fingers aching now that she had reached the last few rows. Bailey did not really mind. Hair Day was a special day for her, a time she shared one-on-one conversations with each child.

"I can finish up with Sage," Sam volunteered, once again admiring Bailey's patience with the girls. He did not think he could sit so long in one spot making perfect cornrows.

"That'll be great. After I'm done here, I'll finish packing goodies for the girls to share with your mom and dad," Bailey replied. When the girls spent a weekend at their grandparents' house, she supplied the first night's meal.

"Dad loves your chicken gumbo," Sam complimented her. His father requested it year round, not just in the winter when the weather was cold, the traditional time in his family to serve the spicy, steamy food.

"Me, too, Daddy," Sage added, her lips smacking as if she tasted the pungent soup right then. She liked most things spicy, and hot.

Dressed in red shorts and a matching top, Fern snorted at her sister. "You just wanta pick out all the sausage," she declared.

Sage leaned forward in her daddy's arms, enjoying the tightening of his muscles as he held on to her more securely. From her safe perch, she stuck her tongue out at Fern. "Nuh unh."

"Yes, you do," Fern argued, her eyes rolling at her sister's bold-faced lie.

"No, I don't," Sage denied, intent on being contrary.

"Yes, you do."

"No—"

"Girls, girls!" Bailey said, jumping in before a shouting match started. Just then, a weekend alone with Sam sounded more than fine.

Sage stuck her tongue out at her sister who returned the gesture. Both children wanted to get the last word.

Sam chuckled, enjoying the familiar bickering. "It'll be empty around here without you two for a weekend, maybe you should stay home."

Fern instantly retreated from her position, her face angelic, her jet-black eyes an exact replica of her father's. "No way, Daddy. Grandma's takin' us shopping."

"Yeah, Daddy," Sage agreed, backing her sister one hundred percent. "Grandma's gonna get me a new straw hat with a ribbon on it."

"You've got a ton of hats, Sage," Fern scoffed, thinking about the bright colored hats that lined a full shelf on her sister's bedroom wall.

"So?" Sage shot back, getting madder by the second at Fern's superior sounding tone of voice.

"So you don't need anymore," Fern told her, conveniently forgetting she owned a lot of hats herself.

"Do too," Sage argued.

"Do not," Fern denied.

"Do too."

"Do—"

"Girls, that's enough," Sam cut in, using his best no-nonsense voice. "Fern, help Mommy finish the packing. Sage, take a seat while I comb your hair."

"Yes, Daddy," the girls replied in unison. They recognized that even though their dad was nice, he was tough, too. When he said *that's enough,* there was no more conversation.

Bailey blew him a kiss. "I'm off to Fern's room. Holler if you need me."

Sam winked at her, fully aware of the twinkle in her eyes. They both knew he loved to comb their daughters' hair. He marveled its versatility the same way he did Bailey's. He liked the way they changed their hair to fit an occasion by braiding it, twisting it, crimping it, or by wearing it loose. They wore hats when they did not want to fuss with fancy hairstyles, or when it rained outside.

No matter how his special ladies wore their hair Sam loved it, just like he loved Hair Day, the time Bailey set aside every other Saturday for herself and the girls to take care of business. On Hair Day everybody was involved. Sam often washed and dried while Bailey did the combing.

Hair Day was never simply about getting clean hair, Sam mused, as he watched Bailey and Fern take off to pack for the girls' getaway weekend with their grandparents. Hair Day bound the body and safeguarded the mind with strong family ties, ties that affected each family member inside and out. After witnessing a teenager's death, he needed this sense of belonging, the sense of balance his family gave him.

Warming up to his hair combing task, he positioned himself on the sofa with Sage on a mint-colored cushion between his knees on the floor. Sun poured through the sloped glass ceiling above their heads, its energy wrapping around them, binding them together with subtle joy.

Gently, he moved a wide toothed comb through Sage's coarse hair, hair as tough and thick as his own. He parted it into four sections, careful not to tug too hard at her tender scalp.

Selecting a red rubber band from the knick-knack box, he pulled each section through the holder, then divided each hank into halves. He twisted together the sections before securing them with red barrettes. To camouflage the red rubber bands, he wrapped ponytail holders around them, bands with clear beads on the ends. It did not take long.

Sage leaned heavily against her father's right knee as she turned to look up at him. "All finished, Daddy?"

"Yep."

"Can I see what Fern's doin'?"

"Go ahead, pumpkin. I'll put away the hair stuff."

"Okay."

A half smile played at Sam's lips as he watched her run to find her sister. No matter how hard he tried, he could not get the triad of perceiving skills: reason, judgment, and understanding, to help him fathom the teenager's death.

All the strong paternal feelings he felt for his daughters caused him to reflect on the loss suffered by the murdered boy's family. The boy would never smile again at his father the way Sage smiled at him today.

As a fresh wave of despair swept through him, he finished putting away the hair supplies in a large plastic box, then lifted himself from the sofa in order to reach the door of the sunroom. Opening the door, he stepped onto the redwood veranda where a distant view showed rolling hills dotted with California oak and eucalyptus trees.

Moving down the short steps off the veranda to the lawn, he ventured into the herb garden he had planted at Sage's birth as a gift to Bailey. He had begun this tradition when he planted a garden of ferns to celebrate the birth of their first child. A snail shell curve of red brick hemmed in the scented garden, the smallest tip of the curve ending at a weathered wood bench made of willow branches.

Along the inner and outer sides of the curves of red brick grew assorted herbs: lungwort, calendula, mint, rosemary, bergamot, parsley, marjoram, thyme, lemon balm, foxglove, and purple sage. While gardening was not his usual hobby, Sam knew all about what plants grew in the herb patch because he planted them as a loving gift to Bailey.

"Sam?" Bailey called softly from the veranda. "Are you okay?"

He remained where he stood; controlled, distant, tense. "No."

Not surprised by his answer, Bailey moved toward him. Placing her arms about his waist from behind, she nestled her left temple against his back. It felt warm, firm, masculine.

"Ridge just called," she informed him quietly. "He wants to talk to you about what happened last night."

Sam sucked in a sustaining breath. "I'm ready."

Bailey squeezed him. "Good, he has other interviews before he speaks with you. By then the girls will be at your mother's house. I'll make a light lunch. Knowing Ridge, he won't stop to eat before he gets here."

"The girls are gonna miss seeing him."

"Knowing Ridge, he'll be equally disappointed," Bailey agreed. "He'll make someone a good husband one day, just like you're a good husband to me. I love you, Sam."

"And I love you," he answered, his voice heavy, solemn. Although he meant the words, his entire manner was subdued, his eyes smudged with shadow, evidence he had slept little the long night before.

"I'm with you all the way," Bailey told him.

"I'm glad. I'm anxious to talk to Ridge, find out what he's learned since last night."

"I understand that," she assured him, "just don't forget I'm here for you."

Saying nothing, Sam covered Bailey's hands with his heavy palms.

"Daaaddyyy!" Sage hollered at the top of her lungs from the sunroom. "Grandma an' Grandpa's here!"

Bailey looked at the watch strapped to her wrist. "And punctual as usual." Lacing her arm through Sam's she said, "Come on, big fella. We've got some huggin' and kissin' to do. I appreciate the way your parents volunteered to keep the girls for the weekend once they heard about what happened last night."

Taking Bailey's hand, Sam could not remember a time he had not felt secure in his parents' love, a love he treasured the older his own children grew. With his daughters safe in their protection, he could join forces with Bailey to seek justice for the murdered teen.

Six

After his parents left with the girls, Sam stood with Bailey in their kitchen, watching as she finished making spaghetti sauce. When the telephone rang he answered it immediately, his hip against the counter. "Hello?"

A woman's voice drawled in his ear. "Is this Sam Walker?"

"Yes," he answered, his bushy brows drawn together at the caller's hushed voice. The long pause grabbed his attention.

"Hello?" Sam repeated, slightly annoyed. Washing dishes, Bailey rocked a brow up in silent question. Sam seldom spoke harshly to anyone.

"I need to talk to you," the drawling voice demanded.

"Who is this?"

There was another long pause.

"Look," Sam said, "I'm not gonna play games. If you've got something to say, get on with it. Otherwise, I'm hanging up."

"Mmm, forceful, I like that in a man."

Sam ran a hand through the short black waves of his hair. "Lady, you've got three seconds to state your business. One—"

"My oh my, what a temper."

"Two—"

"Okay, okay, I'm Elsie Goddard."

"So?" he asked, registering her change of inflection. She no longer drawled.

"So, I've got some information about the boy who was killed last night."

This time, it was Sam who paused. He stopped breathing, then asked, "What kind of information, and why are you calling me instead of the police?"

The drawl returned. "I don't like cops."

"Lady, if you've got ahold of something important about the murder, tell the authorities and do it quick." His wide lips were pursed tight.

The caller uttered a sly, brief laugh "You sound like an authority. Why don't I just tell you what I think the police ought to know?"

His nerves tensed. "Spit it out."

"Aah, aah, aah," she stalled. "It's got to be face to face."

The problem she presented challenged Sam. "When?"

"Now."

He grabbed a pad and pencil. "Where?"

"My place."

Sam paused, this could be a set up. "I need more facts."

"That's why you're coming to my place, angel. The facts."

This time his pause was short. "Tell me your address."

A slow chuckle released itself from the caller. "A decisive man. I like that, too." Her triumph rang clear.

"The address." It was a command, not a question.

"1814 Swan Road, Trinity City."

"Lady," Sam warned, "this had better be good."

Bailey stepped up to Sam as soon as he hung up the telephone. "You sound angry. What gives?"

Excited about the lead in Earl's case, Sam hauled Bailey flat against his chest. She felt good, real good "A tip about last night."

A dozen alarms rang in Bailey's mind. "You're kidding!" she asked, her face and tone serious. The rapid rate of

Sam's heart against her cheek signaled his keen interest in the melodrama which was slowly revealing itself to them.

"I agree it doesn't sound real, but I'm gonna follow up on the call." His kiss on her forehead was hot, firm, comforting.

"Who called?" Bailey asked, holding him tight. He felt invincible.

"Elsie Goddard."

Bailey searched her practical mind of past catering clients and events. "I've never heard of her."

"She lives in Trinity City."

"That's scary, Sam. Trinity City is where Ridge thinks the skinheads may have come from last night." Anxiety beat a fast tattoo at Bailey's temples. She felt a headache coming on at the base of her skull.

"I know."

"What did the woman say to you?" she asked, tipping her head back in order to see into his eyes. They were brilliant with intensity as he answered her question.

After Sam repeated the conversation, Bailey was indignant. "She called you angel?"

Sam smiled at the look on her oval face. "Yeah."

Bailey released her grip on Sam's waist, then paced the kitchen, her mind whirling with apprehension. "I don't like it."

Sam watched her prowl in rapid, repeat steps. "Her calling me angel or her calling me instead of calling the police?"

"Both, and I'm not being jealous."

Sam leaned the hard muscles of his behind against the counter, ankles crossed, arms akimbo. His dark eyes tracked Bailey's every step. "I know. If these were normal circumstances I would never have listened to the woman for as long as I did. I listened to her because I wanna see those punks nailed." His response was bold, blunt, concise.

Bailey glared at the problem, not the man. Their rela-

ionship was too secure for her to be troubled by a mystery
woman with a secret too confidential to share over the
telephone.

Bailey trusted Sam. She said, "I'm with you on that
score. I mean, this Elsie Goddard sounds like a better lead
than the Thunderbird the skinheads used to make their
getaway."

"That's why I agreed to meet her." No indecision ech-
oed in his statement.

Bailey sat down on a chair in the nook with a thump.
Sam's commitment to solving the murder mystery bound
her close to his side through empathy. "That angel business sounds fresh, unstable even. I don't like that woman's
attitude," she admitted, glad she had words to state her
troubled feelings. She and Sam seldom minced words.

Sam pulled up the chair beside her and straddled it so
that they were face to face. "Calling a strange man at his
home for an instant meeting isn't appropriate either, but
she did it. She obviously took the time to find our number
isn't listed in the public directory. Either she got my name
from the news or she got ahold of our number through a
mutual acquaintance," he surmised, enjoying the easy way
he and Bailey matched wits. Their combined strength was
a tangible force in their cozy kitchen.

Bailey wrinkled her nose in concentration. "I doubt we
share friends."

"I can't think of anybody we know who lives in Trinity
City either, but that doesn't rule out that Elsie Goddard
might know somebody who lives in New Hope. There's a
connection between Trinity City and New Hope, maybe
this Goddard woman is a link."

Bailey pushed her cuticles back with a thumbnail while
she puckered her brow in thought. "It's so convenient."

Sam debated her point. "Earl Stackhouse walking alone
to the minimart during off-hours, a perfect victim for the

skinheads to pounce on and make a fast escape, was con
venient."

"You think the killing was closer to home than we firs
thought?" Bailey asked, her pretty brown eyes solemn.

"I do. The attack on Earl was brief and specific and
quiet, too quiet."

Bailey smoothed a coil of red-brown hair behind one
ear before asking, "What do you mean by quiet?"

Sam's answer came slow but steady. "Earl faced down his
attackers with a grim look, not a questioning look, on his
face. I don't think he was so much scared as he was angry."

Bailey's imagination went wild. "He had to be scared."

"Then why didn't he run?"

"Good question."

"I think he didn't run because he felt he had nothing
to fear."

Bailey could not shake loose the vision of Sam's blood-
ied clothes. "With a gang of skinheads on his back Earl
had to be afraid."

"Not if he knew them. If he knew them, he may have
assumed they were just harassing him and would go away.
I can't get outta my head that he didn't run or scream or
panic. That just doesn't make sense to me."

Bailey stroked Sam's jaw. "I bet that's the real reason
you agreed to meet this Goddard woman. You want to
make sense out of the unusual aspects of this case."

"Yeah, the quiet surrounding Earl's death is a clue that
bothers me."

"It bothers me, too," Bailey admitted. "Why don't I
come with you to the Goddard place?"

"What about the spaghetti sauce you've got going on
the stove?"

She had forgotten all about it. "I'll turn the sauce off."

"If you turn it off now, you'll be under pressure later. I
know how you worry over details when we're expecting
company."

"But the case is important," Bailey argued.

Sam cupped her face and kissed her. "So is your peace of mind. Don't worry, sugar. After I follow up this lead, I'm gonna come back so we can talk things over together. You'll be objective. We'll need that objectivity in order to solve the riddles surrounding Earl's death."

"I didn't think about it like that, but you're right." His judgment was one quality of Sam's character Bailey admired. It was sound and constant, like him.

He kissed her again, only slower this time. "I'll be okay."

Her eyes shut tight, Bailey squeezed him with all her might, then let him go. "Hurry home to me, Sam. I'll be waiting."

Chucking her under the chin, he winked. "Damn, I'm lucky."

Chucking him back she said, "So am I."

Reaching his destination, Sam eased his sedan into the skinny driveway of 1814 Swan Road, home to Elsie Goddard. A quick sniff of the Goddard home pulled the scent of frying chicken into his flared nostrils.

He loved fried chicken, especially fried chicken with biscuits and gravy. The familiar smell reminded him of Bailey. Shaking off the distracting thought, he turned his mind on the task at hand.

The August heat burned Sam's ebony skin a deeper color. He registered the quiet sounds of the old mobile home park located on the outskirts of Trinity City. Children laughed as they played with a long green water hose at the far end of the street, narrow and packed with cars. None of the cars were late models.

An elderly Persian woman sprayed prize yellow roses with insecticide. From the way living room curtains opened in the mobile home across the street from him, Sam guessed a neighbor stood there checking him out.

He saw the less than subtle spying as evidence the neighbors on this street looked out for each other, something he thought was a positive way to live. Sam hoped this unexpected meeting went well. He needed a toehold in his vendetta against the skinheads.

He knocked once, twice, then again before Elsie Goddard's flimsy wooden door opened a crack. A pale blue eye peered suspiciously at him. Sam almost laughed at the big difference between their conversation and their meeting. He doubted his next few minutes would be easy ones.

"Yeah?" a wary female voice asked, the tone cool, unfriendly.

"Elsie Goddard?" he queried, removing his shades.

"Maybe."

Temper shot through Sam in a flash. "Don't play games with me, lady. You called. I'm here. Let's get to it."

Sam watched the flimsy wooden door close briefly to let a rusted chain slip its metal catch. "You're much bigger than I expected," the woman said. "Come in."

The slender woman left the front door open, a clue for the amateur detective she was not relaxed in his company, even though she was in her own home and neighbors were watching. Sam could not tell if she was uptight because she had changed her mind about calling him or because of his size.

What intrigued him most about the white woman was her loss of bravado. He called her on it. "You look guilty."

Her shrug was negligent. "Anybody still breathing is guilty of one thing or another."

Sam's thick brows formed a straight line. "Lady, the only confession I wanna hear is you telling me you don't wanna waste my time. What news do you have about the killing last night?"

She said nothing.

Sam's voice was low, tight. "Look, I wanna keep this

meeting as brief as possible. Just skip to the facts behind our call a short while ago."

The woman's gaze swept the length of him. "Angel, you sound and act so official. You've got everything but the uniform."

His six-foot body electric with restless energy, Sam cut to the chase. "I wanna know about Earl Stackhouse."

"I'm getting to it."

When she said nothing more, Sam wanted to shake her. "I'm outta here." He moved to exit.

She grabbed his arm. "Hold it."

Sam scowled, his broad nose pinched, his lips compressed flat in total concentration. "That's better."

"Now that you're here, I'm not so sure . . ." Her voice trailed away to nothing as she lost the decisive edge to her attitude. Suddenly, she was all fluff, no substance.

Sam reined his temper to prod her one last time. "The murder."

Peering at Sam closely, Elsie motioned for him to sit on her tattered, gold striped sofa. She sat across from him on the arm of a worn-out chair. "I heard about what happened on the news. That's where I got your name."

"And?" Sam prompted, narrowing her inconsistent ways to nerves. A chalk-colored woman in her mid-thirties, Elsie Goddard peered at Sam from lashes so short, so fine, so pale they hardly existed.

She wore cut-off blue jeans and a yellow halter top. Her voice had a soft Southern drawl to it that flowed thick or light during the course of a single conversation. She was also nervous, very nervous. Sam wondered why.

"I saw the description of the, uh, gang," she admitted.

He shut his eyes to mask his excitement. "You know them?"

Elsie gnawed a fingernail while she studied the question. Sam waited her out, his chest tight with tension. He asked himself what Bailey would do in this situation. The answer

was to use her intuition. He did, but in the end decided
that for him, observation worked best.

Sam's hard black eyes missed nothing as they slowly
scanned the living room. It had one long window that
faced the street with its nosy neighbors. He noticed that
Elsie Goddard's mobile home was little more than a rickety
tin shack.

Gold shag carpet matched the gold stripes on the furniture. Scratches marked the old coffee table, scattered
with soap opera newsmagazines. He bet watching daytime
TV was Elsie's hobby.

"I've seen them before," she noted as she moved to the
center edge of her frayed armchair. She was blind to the
fly droning above her ashy right knee, below which her
legs were dry and unshaved. The sight was not a pretty
one for the amateur detective.

"Prior to last night?" His question was gruff.

She gave a short, brittle laugh, the kind of laugh that
made the hair on the knuckles of Sam's big hands stand
on end. "Yes," she answered.

He smiled a little to encourage her to continue. It was
the type of cold, polite smile that failed to reach the bottomless depths of his pitch-black eyes. "Go on."

She grunted as if to say, "Don't rush me." Instead, she
imparted fresh information. "They hang out in Trinity
City."

"Where exactly?"

"Club X."

"Here, in Trinity City?" Sam measured the words slowly,
calmly. His mind was hooked.

"Yep."

"What else?"

"I've heard talk at the club." Again her drawl was di-
minished.

"What kind of talk?"

Elsie looked everywhere but at Sam's face. "Talk about

what happened last night. You know, the boot party. I may now who did it.''

Careful to keep his tone neutral, he asked, ''Do you have names?''

Elsie leaned back on the worn sofa, her slender arms olded beneath her full breasts. Her voice was hard. ''Snake, Bash, Grip.'' The words held an edge to them, a bitter edge.

A chill raced through Sam at the confirmation of the names he described for the police the night before. ''Do you know where they live?''

Almost sullen, Elsie studied the chipped edge of her coffee table. She hesitated before saying, ''No. Bash likes to dance. Snake comes to the club to talk war.''

''What kind of war?''

Propping a bare foot on her left thigh, Elsie watched as the tiny housefly headed off toward the frying chicken in her kitchen. ''Race war.''

''Do you know the gang's true names?''

Elsie shrugged, though her pale blue eyes were cagey. ''No.''

Sam found it hard to believe her. ''Ms. Goddard?''

The drawl resurfaced, evidence of her bravado. ''Don't be so formal, angel. Business between us is private.''

Deep grooves of exasperation showed in Sam's cheeks. ''I won't pretend to know where you're coming from, lady. You call me angel one minute, then clam up the next. I don't like being jerked around. So tell me, why did you step forward?''

Sam knew that even though she divulged helpful clues to the skinhead gang's identity, Elsie was not happy about doing so, perhaps the reason why she failed to provide greater details about her presence at Club X, a nightclub that catered to skinheads.

Elsie stopped playing with her middle finger in order to study her guest. ''I know that dead boy's mama.''

Shocked by the news, Sam's voice deepened, his chest constricted, his pulse beat faster as he registered Elsie's tangible discomfort. "How do you know Earl's mother?"

Elsie lowered her lashes so that her eyes were invisible. "She's a friend of mine."

"How long have you known each other?"

To the amateur detective's surprise, she chuckled. This time, the sound was ugly, nasty, full of spite. "Oh me and Earl's mama go way back."

Sam stared at Elsie, a definite link between New Hope and Trinity City. "I've gotta hell of a reason to believe you know the skinheads personally."

Her blue gaze met his black one. "What if I do?"

"If you do, I wanna know how you know them," Sam demanded, his entire body radiating authority.

Elsie hesitated, as if uncertain of her position. "What an honor to be in the presence of such an astute man. I've met one of the men on several occasions."

"Besides Club X?"

"Uh huh."

"Where?"

She glanced away. "His apartment."

"Which man?"

"Grip."

"I need the address."

Sam cast a thorough, confident eye across the odd woman. "Lady, it was hard, but I've figured out your head game."

She narrowed her blue eyes to slits. "Lay it on me, angel."

He held nothing back. "You like fire so you're playing both ends against the middle. You know Earl's mother and you know the skinheads."

"Never said I didn't."

Sam continued on as if she had never spoken. "You know the skinheads well enough to pick one of them out from a police sketch on the news. It's what you know and won't tell me that's making my hair stand up."

"Funny," she said, "you don't look scared." He looked intimidating—tall, dark, and dangerous—a pure alpha male. She felt a sexual rush.

Her suddenly flushed skin surprised Sam. "You wasted time by coming to me instead of the police."

"No, angel. Anybody who steps between a stranger and a gang is a class act. I guess I wanted to meet a . . . hero."

"How do you know I interrupted the fight last night?" he asked.

Her eyes skittered away. "I watched the news."

"I think it's more." His words were soft, deceptively soft.

His entire attitude chilled and excited Elsie. Everything about him was taboo. "Keep thinking. It's good for you."

"You mean good for the case," he clarified.

"There you go sounding all official again."

The way she vacillated between drawling vamp and cool informant made Sam uneasy. "You don't make sense."

She tsked. "If I'm not making sense, angel, it means you aren't listening. I called you up because you're a man of action."

"So are the cops," he countered.

"I don't like cops."

Sam was nobody's fool. "You must be involved in some way, which means you've got something personal you wanna hide."

Elsie lifted a brow in a show of sarcasm. "Don't we all?"

"Anything else?" he prompted, standing to leave.

She watched him rise to his full height. "Only for you, angel."

"What is it?" he asked rudely, hating the games she was playing. He liked the way Bailey always spoke her mind.

"Grip's address."

Sam kept his surprise under wraps as he pulled a business card from his wallet. She provided the pencil, its top chewed off. He was careful not to touch that very personal part of her pencil with his fingers.

His movements fluid, Sam extended a hand to her, ending their meeting. She gave him the creeps. "Call me if you think of anything else. The leads are good. I'll pass them on to the police."

"Do that," Elsie said, though her tone was less than gracious.

On impulse, Sam decided to make one more stop before heading home to Bailey, Grip's apartment in Trinity City.

Seven

Outside Grip's apartment, Sam cased the complex from the driver's seat of his sedan, parked across the street. He was pumped by the forward movement in the Stackhouse case, the memory of Earl's murder never far from his mind.

It was less than twenty-four hours since the murder, and already Sam possessed a vital lead. His heart beating steady, his nerves under control, he focused on the task, amateur sleuthing skills at the ready.

The eight buildings that comprised Grip's apartment complex were quiet as were the streets that bordered it. The building was at least thirty years old. It was dark gray with light gray trim. Twenty-foot trees dotted the property. There were no flowers. The green grass was recently mowed.

As he watched, a thin man with a scraggly beard left the apartment building. The number posted at the end of the building was seven, Sam's lucky number. He grinned, unnoticed by the departing tenant, who was walking off in a hurry to catch a fast-approaching city bus.

Once the city bus left its scheduled stop, Sam popped the door latch on his sedan. Stepping away from the car, he locked it. Instead of returning the keys to his pocket, he used them to open the trunk of his car.

Inside the trunk he kept a bag of emergency supplies

which he held on to in case of a roadside mishap. Inside the white plastic shopping bag was a flashlight, batteries, flares, a cardboard HELP sign, a screwdriver, a wrench, a few rags, and a pair of all-purpose rubber gloves. He kept the gloves in the car for Bailey. He smiled slightly at the gloves' current unexpected use.

Sam donned the gloves, slipped the screwdriver into his left front pocket, locked the trunk, and put the keys in his right front pocket. He had no need to glance twice at the business card with Grip's apartment unit number scrawled across it. The unit number was embedded in his mind. Sam walked to Building Three of the Redwood Arms as if he did it every day.

His ears tuned in to the distant, familiar sounds of honking cars, droning insects, and rustling tree leaves, Sam studiously ignored the heat that pelted his body until it sweat. Reaching unit 852 of Building Three, he tried to peek through the curtains at the window. The curtains blocked his view completely. He saw nothing between the narrow space that separated the left side of the curtain from the right side. The lack of interior light spurred him on.

He rang the bell, thankful for the form-fitting latex gloves. It was not the first time he would break into a suspect's home. He did it once before with Bailey during their first stint as private citizens turned detectives. In the present moment, Sam missed her company something fierce.

No one answered the multiple rings to the doorbell. Sam considered this an excellent sign because he had no excuse lined up for either his presence or the rubber gloves that covered his hands. Sweat trickled down his back. He ignored it.

Taking the screwdriver from his left front pocket, he jimmied the wooden door, its gray paint peeling from the harsh rays of the sun. It took scarcely a heartbeat to separate the old door from its jamb. With no hesitation, Sam entered the premises.

Once inside the apartment, he shut the door with a snap; he had popped the door open without breaking the jamb. Standing quietly, he listened. No sound penetrated the silence. Moving across the studio apartment to the dinette area, he pulled a green plastic chair from the two-man table, wedging the sturdy chair beneath the doorknob for extra privacy.

It did not take him long to see the bare bones of the small apartment. His visual survey showed him there was a kitchenette, a minuscule area for a dinette set, a living space just big enough for a sofa that doubled as a bed. A brief hallway led to a closet and a bathroom.

Everything about the one room apartment was ordinary, including the mess. Piles of dirty laundry stood in one corner of the living room. An old pizza box sat on the dinette table, as did two empty beer cans. The pizza crust inside the box was hard, indicating to Sam it had not been purchased recently.

Dishes sat unwashed in the kitchen sink. There was one glass, one plate, one cutlery set. The contents of the refrigerator were sparse. There was a six-pack of beer, a small can of coffee, a box of raisins, lunch meat, bread, condiments, and a rotten green apple. Sam deduced Grip lived alone. He decided to search the place, one square foot at a time.

He began his search in the bathroom. The bathtub was black with dirt, the enamel on the cracked tub long gone. The white soap in the ceramic soapdish was old and cracked, too. Sam stood on the edge of the bathtub in order to check the short ledge below the single window. He found nothing but a cobweb and a thick layer of dirty grime. The window had mildew on it.

Sam removed the shower curtain rod from the beige wall. He unscrewed the ends off the shower rod, peering inside either end. As with the windowsill, he discovered nothing unusual.

Not having any idea what to look for in the skinhead's apartment, Sam looked at anything and everything, hoping to find some clue of Grip's true identity, some evidence that might link him squarely to the murder scene.

He opened the medicine cabinet. Inside the white metal box were three metal shelves lined with medicine and toiletry items. The bottom seam of the toothpaste was rolled nearly to the cap. The toothbrush was new, but dusted with dried brown food particles.

There were two bottles of over-the-counter pain killers, one bottle of vitamins, and a paper package of cold medicine. Sam opened each bottle, finding them all nearly empty. The cold medicine had only one capsule missing.

Sam checked under and around the toilet. It stank. He lifted the lid from the back of the white colored commode. He looked inside, finding nothing. He lifted the rug from the floor in front of the bathtub. Again he found nothing.

Returning everything close to where he found it, Sam left the bathroom to search the closet in the hallway. After a fifteen-minute scramble through every pocket, shoe, bag, and suitcase, he found exactly what he had found in the bathroom, nothing.

He went to the kitchen next. Despite the stifling, hot air inside the studio apartment, Sam checked every inch of space inside, on top of, behind, and beside the refrigerator. There was nothing at all unusual, only spiders whose webs he disturbed, invading their territory.

Methodically, Sam searched the freezer. Inside the freezer was a half empty carton of neapolitan ice cream. The inside of the carton was frosted with ice. Like all the other food in Grip's apartment, the ice cream was stale. The cabinets in the kitchen yielded nothing.

The dinette set was sticky with old beer and pizza crumbs. There were no taped envelopes beneath the flat surface of the tabletop, nor beneath the twin chairs that belonged to the table.

The trash can yielded a frayed *Playboy* magazine, crumpled dinner napkins, a classified ad from the employment section of the local newspaper, one junk circular, and two recent bills: one from Pacific Bell, the other from Pacific Gas & Electric.

The amounts on the bills were minimal; the name on the bills was significant. Grip's true name was Douglas Abernathy. Sam pocketed the bills. He felt jubilant, proud, and more than a little bit cocky. He could scarcely wait to show Bailey.

He had one place left to search: the area surrounding the sofa which doubled as a pull out bed. Sam removed the brown fabric cushions from the sofa. There were three of them. He pulled out the sofa bed.

A thin, army-style blanket covered the worn cotton sheets on the thin mattress. Sam stripped the bed, finding nothing. Lifting the mattress, he turned it on its side to check the metal frame of the hideaway bed. He found a surprise: an artist's pad, the type of pad found in drugstores beside school supplies.

Sam returned the mattress to the bed. He folded the sheets and blanket, set them squarely on the bed. He removed the case from the standard size pillow, finding nothing. He set the pillow beside the sheets and the army blanket. He closed up the sofa, returned the cushions to their proper place, and sat down.

He opened the portfolio. A series of pencil sketches graced every single page in the oversize paper tablet. Every sketch was of a single woman in various poses. In every pose the woman was dressed. Sam pulled one sketch from the artist's tablet, folded the sketch into fourths, and placed the sketch in his back pocket. He placed the pad on the center cushion of the sofa; his calling card.

On the way to his sedan, Sam felt on top of the world. He had three pieces of evidence and two dramatic clues:

the true name of one suspect plus the pencil sketch of another—the female driver of the skinheads' getaway car.

Sam's next stop before going home was at a Trinity City phone booth. The phone booth was located at an Arco gas station six blocks away from the Redwood Arms apartment complex. Opening the directory, he scanned the white residential pages until he found the listings for Abernathy.

There were three Abernathy residents in Trinity City, one of them Douglas, aka Grip. Jotting down the other two names, addresses, and telephone numbers on the back of a fresh business card, Sam returned the phone book to its slot inside the public booth.

Sam was the only person in the sun baked parking lot with a bounce in his step. His dark eyes glittering with pleasure, he whistled all the way to his car.

Meanwhile, Bailey puttered around the house waiting for Sam to come home. Methodically, she checked the stock of staple foods she kept in the pantry. On her list of lined paper, she added flour, sugar, cornmeal, cream of tarter, and poppy seeds. She also needed vegetable shortening and red wine vinegar.

Humming Al Green's classic hit song, "Love and Happiness," Bailey tried not to worry about Sam. She had expected him home by now, the reason his extended absence set her nerves jangling. She wished now she had turned the spaghetti sauce off and insisted on going with him.

Determined to control her unease in a positive way, Bailey concentrated on straightening up her home for company. The very ordinary, routine chores of vacuuming, sweeping, and dusting calmed her; they brought order to her thoughts as well as her home.

The spacious old farmhouse formed the center of the love she shared with Sam, and was the place where they extended their love to family and friends. Preparing her home for company was a welcome custom.

After putting her cleaning paraphernalia in a long cupboard in the laundry room, Bailey washed her hands at the laundry sink, then creamed them with the cocoa butter she kept on a handy shelf which also held laundry washing aids. Already, she felt restored. If Sam was in trouble, he would have called home as he had Friday night after the murder.

Finding solace in the subtle peace of her home, Bailey started humming. As was her habit, the humming turned into singing, her voice loud and off-key as she cut loose with Steve Wonder's oldie but goody, "Skeletons," from the *Characters* compact disc:

> *Skeletons in your closet*
> *Itchin' to come outside*
> *Messin' with your conscience*
> *In a way your face can't hide*

Bailey believed that every event in a person's life was connected, that nothing happened by chance but by a divine order of things. As hard as it was for her to accept Earl's murder, she wondered at how his death was connected to a larger reality, a reality based on a truth, but bound to be both simple and ugly. She had learned this from her first foray as an amateur detective.

In that case, she had been the main person asking questions, which had stirred up more trouble than she ever imagined would come her way. Now that Sam was doing the asking, stirring up already heightened emotions, all she wanted to do was protect him.

She knew from close personal experience that delving into other peoples' secret lives was risky business, and she wanted to protect Sam as he had once protected her. How could she control what happened to him without creating a conflict between them as a couple? she wondered. Asking him to wait for the police was too ineffectual a strategy for an active man to take.

Telling him to stop his investigation was like standing in front of a moving freight train. The train would move on, but the aftermath would be as ugly as the initial conflict. In order to best support Sam, Bailey decided to keep a level head.

While Sam was strong, and full of a commitment based on honor and a keen sense of responsibility, a deep rage burned constantly within him. A child had died by violent, racist hands. Whether she understood his full reasons or not, Bailey knew he needed to avenge that death. No way could she stop him, nor truthfully, did she want to try.

Her decision made, Bailey set about making a late breakfast. Although the girls had bowls of cold cereal after they woke up, neither she nor Sam were inclined to eat at that time. Combing heads, cleaning house, and preparing for company now had Bailey's stomach rumbling.

Working with systematic precision, she set about making baking powder biscuits. Sam loved the light, feathery, melt-in-your-mouth treats. She served them with chicken and gravy for dinner, but for breakfast she served them with sausage and eggs.

From the pantry she gathered flour, baking powder, salt, sugar, and shortening. From the refrigerator she secured a carton of low-fat milk. In a large glass bowl, she sifted the dry ingredients together.

Taking two knives from the cutlery drawer, she cut the shortening into the dry ingredients. She raked the knives back and forth like scissors until the bread mixture clumped into tiny bits.

She added milk to the bread mixture, stirring it with a fat spoon until it formed a ball. Dusting her hands with flour, she removed the dough from the mixing bowl, placed it on a floured cutting board and kneaded it lightly six times.

With her hands, she pressed the dough in a circle that was roughly a half-inch thick. Using a metal biscuit cutter, she punched out the dough, placing the circles on an un-greased cookie sheet. She repeated the rolling, cutting, and punching process until the cookie sheet was full. She placed the biscuits in the oven for fifteen minutes.

While the biscuits baked, Bailey scrambled eggs in a me-dium size mixing bowl. She put the eggs in a non-stick pan, coated with a pat of butter for flavor. She added moz-zarella and cheddar cheeses to the eggs, along with salt and pepper. Right after the eggs had cooked, she heard Sam walk through their living room door.

"Sugar, I'm home!" he hollered, his long strides taking him straight to the kitchen that smelled so good. Sam was hot, excited, starving, and anxious to see Bailey.

"It's about time!" she hollered back, thankful they were together again.

Deciding that sausage would take too long to cook, Bailey returned the package to the refrigerator, choosing thin ham slices instead. One thing she had learned sleuth-ing her way through a murder mystery was that she had to be flexible and go with the flow.

After breakfast, Sam helped Bailey straighten the kitchen. After they had put away the last of the dishes, he led her to the living room. Neither one of them had said a word about the mystery woman, or what Sam had dis-covered after meeting her. They needed this peaceful, grounding time together.

Once they were seated on the couch side by side, Bailey snuggled closer to his body, her brown eyes half-closed as she savored all the wonderful feelings Sam aroused in her. She felt protected, wanted, loved. She kissed his shoulder.

Nuzzling his nose against the rose scent of her hair, he whispered, "I missed you too, sugar."

"What was the Goddard woman like?" Bailey asked, knowing it was time to discuss Sam's absence that morning.

Sam recalled the chalk-colored woman with the ashy legs. "She was rude, weird."

"Did she tell you anything of importance?" Bailey asked, touched by a sense of horror.

"She had a drawl she turned on and off depending on the way she felt."

Bailey tried to understand. "Like an accent that thickens with emotion?"

"Yeah. The drawl was heavy when she felt confident, light when she felt she had to be careful about what she said."

Bailey evaluated Sam's statement. "She was cautious then."

"Very. She also had a guilty air about her."

Bailey found this interesting. "The guilt implies personal involvement, which could also explain her secrecy."

"That's what I think, too."

"Obviously she got our number from the directory."

Sam nodded.

Bailey tried to fit the pieces together. "Do you believe her?"

"Yeah. She didn't strike me as a liar, even though she behaved in a strange way. She sought me out, which means she had something eating at her, something she wasn't comfortable about taking straight to the police."

Bailey's tone was cynical. "Not wanting to go to the police seems underhanded."

"I thought so too, until she told me she was friends with Earl's mother."

Bailey's blood felt icy, leaving her cold. "No way."

"She wouldn't go into details, but her declaration proves that Earl probably died at the hands of somebody he knows. Elsie Goddard associates with skinheads in Trinity City. She lives in Trinity City and personally knows Earl's mother. This connection is specific."

"Maybe Earl's death was a hit."

Sam negated the idea immediately. "I don't think so, because the death was so public. I believe the skinheads planned to beat Earl, not kill him."

All sorts of possibilities blew through Bailey's mind. Every single one of them was ugly. She focused on the victim. "Okay, did she give you any idea who might have wanted to hurt Earl?"

"Yeah."

"Who?" She awaited his answer with suspended breath.

"Doug Abernathy."

Bailey leaned her back against the sofa. "Never heard of him."

"Doug Abernathy is a skinhead called Grip. Grip was at the beating, something Goddard says she figured out after seeing his police drawing on TV. She did not claim she recognized anyone else."

"You only have her word that Doug Abernathy is Grip."

Sam felt jubilant. "I've got proof."

"How?"

"Goddard gave me Grip's address. She knows him from a skinhead nightclub called Club X in Trinity City. I went to Grip's apartment, broke in, searched the place, and came up with two vital pieces of evidence: confirmation of Grip's true identity and an artist's sketch of the driver of the Thunderbird."

Bailey took his breaking-and-entering stint in stride. She had instigated a break-in once herself. "Tell me about the search."

Sam told her about the detailed hunt. "I learned from you that clues are often hidden in secret, yet obvious places. Without you beside me, I decided to search one square foot at a time."

Bailey laughed softly, her expression wry. "We aren't exactly bumbling crooks anymore, are we?"

Gently, Sam squeezed her hand. "No, I would never have broken into Grip's apartment if so much weren't at stake. At any minute I expect a riot to break out in this town. If somebody doesn't snag those skinheads soon it's gonna be war between New Hope and Trinity City."

"Race war."

"That's what Elsie Goddard said. The idea bothered me so much, I went straight to a Trinity City phone booth to get a listing of local Abernathys."

"Let's check them out."

Sam pulled the list from his back pocket and handed it to her. His grin had a bit of a wolfish look to it. "I figured you were gonna say that."

"Oh, that boy never gave a fig about schooling," Martha Abernathy explained about her son, Doug. She was the third Abernathy on the list. The number three was Bailey's favorite number.

After the Walkers had explained what they wanted, Martha talked to them on the porch of her one-story bungalow. Wisteria climbed across the porch railing. They all stood in a semi-circle as if it were a comfortable seventy degrees outside instead of one hundred.

"How so?" Bailey asked the chatty woman. She and Sam agreed she would do all the questioning while Sam simply observed, his entire demeanor on guard for anything unusual.

Her short, round body jiggling with excess body weight, blue-haired Martha said, "Why, he's a hoodlum, honey."

Bailey swatted a mosquito off her arm. "Will you explain?"

Martha's gray eyes squinted in deep thought. "When Dougie was just a little boy, say four years old or so, I tried my best to get him to read some. You know, get a hang of the alphabet at least.

"Heavens, we had a ton of books because my husband, that's Big Doug, didn't believe in us watching TV. Why, before it was popular, Big Doug knew TV rotted a person's brain. That's why he had me teach Dougie his letters way before we put him in regular school."

Bailey still did not have the answer she wanted. "Where does the hoodlum part come into play?" she plainly asked.

"Well, Dougie just read every darn thing he could get his little hands on. He even memorized stuff. You know, the nursery rhymes, even stuff from the bible. After awhile he just . . . stopped." Martha stared off into space as her high, brittle voice trailed away. She appeared to be in her late sixties.

"Gradually?" Bailey probed.

"No, he just quit. Bam. Just like that." Martha played with the red button on the front of her flowered house-coat.

"Why?" Bailey asked, thankful Martha was so willing to cooperate. She and Sam needed her help.

Martha sighed, her wide gray eyes very clear. "He de-cided he was grown. After that happened, school was just something to do. For Dougie, it was a plain waste of his time. I dunno, I guess me and Big Doug just spoiled him. You know, letting him read the bible and all by the time he was five. Why, he got too big for his boots that's all."

Bailey struggled to follow Martha's less than straightfor-ward train of thought. "You're saying school bored him?"

Martha's big gray eyes looked Bailey up and down. "Yes, honey, that's exactly what I'm saying."

A few seconds of silence passed before Bailey posed her next question. She swatted the mosquito away twice, sur-prised Martha appeared content to stand in the heat. "How did you handle it?" she asked.

Martha sighed once more. "Well, Big Doug just beat the pants off him. Pretty soon Dougie didn't care about that at all. He was so . . . restless. He just plain didn't care about nothing."

Bailey did a quick mental calculation. "He was only what? Ten?"

Martha's high, brittle voice was grave. "A very mature ten. Why, Dougie wouldn't mind his teachers just like he wouldn't mind me. He was late to class, played sick at home, and picked fights in between school and home. He was difficult."

"An only child?" Bailey guessed.

Martha shifted her large slippered feet against the green outdoor carpet that covered her cement porch. "Why, yes, honey. Dougie was about all me and Big Doug could handle."

Bailey looked at Sam, who leaned against the porch railing. He was staring at Martha as if she were something rare. "Where is Mr. Abernathy now?" Bailey asked.

Martha's florid face was matter-of-fact. "Dead in his grave, honey, just plain dead in his grave."

Bailey's brown eyes grew gentle, as did her tone. "I'm sorry."

Martha glanced at Sam. Until now, she had not paid him much attention. "Don't be. He died of throat cancer from all them cigarettes he smoked. By the time the Good Lord called his name, Big Doug was ready. So was I."

A sudden thought jolted Bailey to ask, "So your son wasn't close to his father?"

"No, and to tell you the truth, I only see Doug on Christmas and Mother's Day. He does send money now and then. I prefer it that way." Her voice held a ring of truth to it.

Bailey could not imagine only wanting to see her grown children twice a year, not if they lived close by. "Why?" Her voice expressed her bewilderment.

Martha looked down at her fuzzy red slippers. "Well, Dougie is sullen now that he's older."

Bailey frowned. "How so?"

Martha's face showed displeasure. "The boy is sneaky, that's what I mean. He can be mad as a hornet, but instead of confronting somebody with his anger, he'll hang on to it while he thinks up some way to get even with the person he's mad at. No, there ain't much that's direct about Dougie."

Bailey pursued this line of thought. "Did he have any close friends growing up?"

Again Martha glanced at Sam, who maintained a neutral expression on his face. At first glance, he looked lazy. Bailey saw that his pitch black eyes were crisply alert. "One, and he's a bad seed for sure," Martha replied.

"Do you remember the person's name?" Bailey prompted, fresh anxiety building inside her belly.

Martha Abernathy was a gold mine of information. Bailey guessed she did not receive many visitors, which was why she was so talkative with virtual strangers, people with a slim, negative, connection to her wandering son.

"I sure should, honey. Dougie's best friend growing up was his friend, Tate Jones. Tate was rotten back then and he's rotten now." Martha shook her blue-rinsed head in disgust.

"What was Tate like?"

Martha motioned for Bailey to join her on the porch swing. It rocked gently beneath their weight. Sam remained where he stood against the porch rail. "Strictly thug material," the elderly woman answered. "He and my son hooked up at about age twelve, puberty. Somehow Tate got into drugs. I hear he's into one of them white gangs, you know the kind honey, them KKK gangs." Martha said the letters KKK in a whisper.

Completely focused on the conversation, Bailey was as oblivious to the heat as Martha was. "Is Doug in the gang too?"

Martha snorted. "Wouldn't surprise me none. Last time I saw Tate and Dougie together it was a year ago. They were talking about some white gang called Satan's Magic. Can you believe that name?

"I told them boys I didn't want no devil worshippers in my house. They just laughed at what I said and went on about their business. I've seen Dougie twice since that day, but Tate ain't never been back which is fine with me."

A subtle nod from Sam signaled to Bailey it was time to conclude their interview with Grip's mother. "I appreciate your honesty, Mrs. Abernathy," Bailey said. "I know this conversation couldn't have been easy for you."

Martha tsked. "Honey, I lost my little boy a long time ago. Dougie's a man now. If he's done wrong, why, he's just got to pay. Fair is fair, I say."

Sam extended his hand to Martha once Bailey had joined his side. "We thank you."

Martha looked at Sam's big, rough hand a long time before she took it within both her own. She said, "Tate's play name was Bash because he was always breaking things up. You know, like Bam Bam on the Flintstones cartoon. I kind of feel in my heart, you two are caring people. I'm just sorry for all the trouble going on in your town. I've been to New Hope. It's a pretty place."

On impulse, Bailey gave the short woman a hug. "Stop by our home any time," she offered. "You're welcome."

Martha returned Bailey's hug, then stepped back. "With all this race tension going on, and your suspicion my Dougie might be part of the problem, I'm touched you'd offer such a thing. Bless you child."

On the way to their car, Sam laced his fingers through Bailey's, saying softly in the smooth shell of her ear, "I love you."

Eight

Meanwhile, Detective Ridge Williams marveled at the beautiful day, a day certain to remain as terribly hot as the day before. In his office earlier than usual, he worried about his friend, Sam. He worried that Sam might track Earl Stackhouse's murderers himself, if a lawful resolution to the conflict was not reached quickly.

From the experience he had gained as a police officer, Ridge knew it was not the first time a law-abiding man like Sam would turn vigilante, for the sake of honor or for the satisfaction of revenge. He also understood the consequences of vigilante behavior. If Sam were to commit battery, or worse, he would be no better than the criminals he sought.

Wrestling with the blues, Ridge opened the almond-colored mini-blinds inside his office, which was devoted to his business use alone. The small space exuded order and control, a reflection of the detective's character.

The office overlooked the tiny concrete terrace where New Hope Township Police Department employees often took break or lunch. Ridge seldom joined the revolving crowd, often eating his meals on the run or at his desk to get the most use of his time.

This early in the morning the terrace was empty. The standard office work crew was down to the weekend wire, the two days of the week when off-duty personnel were

free to share time with close family and special friends
Special friends made him think of the Walkers.

The image of Sam and Bailey, a couple with children
hobbies, and goals together, renewed his hunger for the
same thing. The couple was secure and compatible with
each other while Ridge was married to his job. He no
longer wanted to live this way.

He was a cop, he reminded himself, a man somewhat
jaded when it came to human nature, a reason some
women he met were turned off, once they discovered his
career. It did not take these women long to figure out that
his job was not as exciting as it looked on television.

Those women who were intrigued enough to date him
more than a few times eventually moved on from the
relationship, once the novelty of his career wore off and
the reality of it set in. He worked long, unpredictable
hours.

Since becoming a police officer, Ridge had lost his rose
colored view of ordinary people and regular society. From
experience, he knew crime occurred when evil lurked be
hind familiar eyes. This happened in many cases of violent
crime.

Shoving his hands in his pockets, he turned away from
deep thoughts to study his recently painted office. Or
derly and efficient, its white walls were covered in area
maps. Beside the maps were department bulletins. Next
to the bulletins were certificates of achievement. Near the
certificates were police team photographs; beginning in
Portland, Oregon, ending in New Hope, California. His
long career was highlighted with awards and stellar suc
cesses.

His desk was dark gray metal with a walnut veneer top. He
dusted it every other week, after watering his ivy plants. He
spent more time in his office at the police station than he did
at home. This state of affairs had troubled him of late.

As Ridge's eyes perused the room, someone knocked

on the door before coming inside. It was Carlyle Higgins, looking fit in navy slacks with a light blue shirt, dark belt, and dark shoes. Like Ridge, he moved with the confidence of a powerfully built, successful man.

Carlyle asked his friend, "Ready for b-b-briefing?" It was Carlyle who informed the Stackhouse family of their loss. Earl was survived by his parents and a sibling.

"As ready as I'll ever be."

Wanting to keep the meeting informal, Ridge motioned to the two matching chairs in front of his desk with a wave of a sculpted, milk chocolate-colored hand. He took one chair, Carlyle took the other, his face riddled with fatigue. It had been a long, hot, troublesome weekend.

"I've rarely missed a d-d-day of work in my life, but today I wanted to stay at home with my wife and kids."

"I can see how a family might make this job more bearable."

"You c-c-can say that again. It seems like boys dying by violent crime are getting younger every year."

"I think so, too."

Like Carlyle, Ridge opened a manila file folder containing field investigation notes. He asked, "The parents positively identified the body?"

A nerve twitched on Carlyle's face, just above his right cheek. "Yes, Mrs. Stackhouse broke down completely. I don't believe there's a more awful sound on earth than a mother grieving for her dead child. I c-c-could hardly stand it."

Ridge understood. "We'll catch that gang," he promised, as much to himself as to his friend. "They know they left evidence at the crime scene," he added, referring to the baseball bat. "Any news from forensics?" The forensic scientists were the experts in charge of isolating the fingerprints, hair, and fibers the field team had recovered in relation to Earl's murder from the conven-

ience store parking lot. They were specialized, dedicated
people.

Carlyle had just left the forensic lab, located in the windowless basement of the police station. "Forensics is working d-d-double time. Everybody at the station knows
people are fired up over what happened last night."

Ridge bent a steel paperclip between his right index finger and thumb; the act showed Carlyle that Ridge's nerves
were frayed. They had worked late the night before and
would probably work late this night.

"Don't you know it. The news media is keeping the pot
boiling. Earl's body was scarcely cold before his name hit
the tube. It's unbelievable."

Carlyle knew Ridge spoke the truth, and he agreed.
"Until now I'd only thought of skinheads as fairly harmless
people, just young k-k-kids trying to look tough."

Ridge felt the sharp stab of anger in his stomach. "So
did I, until the late eighties when my cousin, Darius, got
the wrong end of a boot party."

Carlyle was surprised. "Boot party?"

"A boot party is when skinheads stomp someone until
they are unconscious or dead. It's a ritual that sometimes
starts with racial taunts, and ends with a beating by a crude
instrument, such as a baseball bat or a strong strip of chain.
Like Earl Stackhouse, my cousin didn't survive the beating."

Carlyle grimaced. "I'm sorry. Where d-d-did this happen?"

Ridge stared into the distance, his chest constricted with
old pain. Darius was his first cousin on his father's side of
the family. Together they had learned to ride bikes, played
in Little League, and gone to their senior prom.

"Portland, Oregon," he answered Carlyle at last, his
voice soft as warm butter. "My cousin's death is what got
me to join the police force. In the police force I learned

about WAR; White Aryan Resistance, and AYM; Aryan Youth Movement."

"I've heard of them."

"Then you know that both of those right wing groups are stronger, older, more organized warrior groups than skinheads will ever be. It wasn't until a year ago that I was able to get a gang task force started in New Hope."

Since coming to New Hope, Ridge tried to establish the need for gang awareness within the ranks of his department. He was surprised to find them complacent about the subject. His superiors felt that New Hope, a fairly small town, would always be a source of multicultural pride, not a hotbed of gang activity.

The nerve in Carlyle's cheek twitched again. "It's a shame we even need a t-t-task force. Some people think that because we live in California and not a small town in the Midwest or the South, that racism is not around. It is, it's just better hidden."

"I agree with you, but not everybody does. I don't walk around thinking in terms of color, but racial intolerance is an unresolved issue in this country. The murder last night confirms it."

"Skinheads in New Hope. I just c-c-can't believe it."

"It's hard to take. There are two distinct groups: the racist skinheads who probably killed Earl, and the antiracist group called Sharps; Skinheads against Racial Prejudice."

"I've heard of them. Both groups wear the military look, buzzed heads, thick b-b-boots, and camouflage, but not always. Some wear straight leg jeans or T-shirts."

"Also," Ridge added, "members of both groups tend to be under twenty-five."

"The witnesses said the music the g-g-gang played from their car was loud."

"Skinhead music is loud all right," Ridge responded. "The stuffs loud and deadly. I remember lines from a song I've heard by Ken Death:

Line them up against a wall.
Shoot them watch them die.
I love to hear the agony.
They vomit, scream, and cry.

Carlyle shook his head, appalled by the lyrics. "If the skinheads had guns last night, there may have been more victims."

Ridge drew his thick brows together in a straight line. "I think so too. Baseball bats are skinhead weapons of choice because they're easy to swing, easy to buy."

Carlyle's baritone voice simmered with anger. "There aren't any laws against carrying a b-b-bat."

"Right, the good thing about wood versus aluminum bats is that they're often inscribed with information about the owner, details helpful in court."

"Names?"

"Yes, and racial slurs."

The beginnings of a smile touched the outer corners of Carlyle's mouth, though the smile did not reach his hazel eyes. "I bet that g-g-goes over real well with a jury."

Ridge caught his friend's meaning. "It does help them to see skinheads as more than odd looking, but harmless people. Granted, there are shades of involvement within any organization. For instance, some people who join skinhead gangs join because they want a family setting, even though it's a negative one. Some join simply to rebel against family and church."

Carlyle tallied the possibilities. "I can see how lonely, confused kids might b-b-be lured into gangs for protection. Runaway kids from the streets, kids from rough schools, and kids from t-t-tough neighborhoods are easy targets for just about any kind of gang, regardless of race."

Ridge eased his body against the back of his chair, his long legs stretched in front of him. "It happens more than you'd think. The people I've learned about on both sides of the skinhead coin, racist and nonracist, are largely joining for reasons rooted in low self esteem."

Carlyle's thoughts were so grave his eyes were illegible to anyone other than his wife, Rowena. "It sounds to me as if on the surface, racist skinheads and nonracist skinheads are the same, yet underneath the military look, each g-g-gang is as individual as its members."

"You're right. I've discovered that gangs create their own subculture, a culture that weeds out groups of people they don't find suitable to their philosophy."

Carlyle stretched out his shoulders. They were fit from weight lifting in the garage with his son four nights a week. "They've got too much p-p-power."

Ridge pursued the topic on an elementary level. "Many gangs I've studied are built around people who feel powerless on their own. As a gang, the skinheads are perceived as tough guys."

"The tough guy image is enhanced by the military clothes, the obscene music, and the power-in-numbers mentality. I suppose that in their minds, their b-b-biggest power is the color of their skin," Carlyle said.

"I had a harder time than you'd guess convincing our superiors that skinhead gangs are as much a threat to mainstream society as are the more well-publicized black gangs, such as the Crips or the Bloods," Ridge said.

Carlyle frowned in concern. "Our superiors are b-b-black."

Ridge understood the dilemma. "Black and secure. New Hope has a far lower homicide rate than San Jose, San Francisco, Oakland, or Richmond. Gang related activities, including the drug trade, aren't as keen here as they are in those other, larger local cities."

"True."

"Until recently, our superiors were too complacent, too willing to go along with the general idea that New Hope will always be a safe place for people of color."

"That's how the town got its name. It was supposed to bring new hope to p-p-people who wanted to succeed in the West," Carlyle said.

"I didn't know that."

"I know you got our superiors to change their minds when they didn't want to deal with the g-g-gang task force issue. We never talked in d-d-detail about how you pulled it off." They had begun working together after the task force was in place.

Ridge remembered the time, the meetings, the subtle pressure he had expended in realizing his long-term goal. "Research. Statistics. In the mid-eighties skinheads in Portland started out as punk rockers, people I considered strange looking but harmless until my cousin's death."

A graphic image of Earl entered Carlyle's brain. "I thought the same thing. The stripe of hair d-d-down the middle of a bald head, the green hair, blue hair, pink hair, whatever."

"It's true they don't always fit into the punk fashion stereotype."

"I guess you could say that every generation we've ever known had a subculture that spoke for the wild at heart. In the t-t-twenties there were flappers. In the sixties there were hippies."

"And through it all, racist hate crimes prevailed."

Resolve strengthened Carlyle's voice. "Well, last night's crime won't go unpunished. I've got names of key witnesses, along with b-b-brief notes, about what they saw."

Ridge snapped fresh lead into his mechanical pencil. "Tell me their names."

Carlyle reeled off names without double checking his notes; he had done this prior to his meeting with Ridge. "Barbara Johnson, Benjamin Reilly, Quentin Jasper, and Sam Walker. A woman named Elsie Goddard c-c-called this morning with a tip."

"Good." Once Ridge recorded the addresses as well as

the initial statements of the witnesses, he jotted down other pertinent information from Carlyle's preliminary notes.

He did this in longhand as he had at the Jasper Mini Mart crime scene, the Stackhouse home, the morgue, and as he would later at the quiet of his cluttered office desk in the New Hope Township police station. Carlyle's briefing was thorough yet concise, the way Ridge liked it.

Nine

At the close of Ridge's meeting with Carlyle, Sam rambled about his garage as Bailey stuffed a load of laundry into the washing machine. His body was a solid mass of tough muscle over hard bone. He had changed into charcoal-colored walking shorts and a light gray polo shirt.

With a few hours left to count until Ridge's arrival for an eyewitness interview follow up, and for an update on the official hunt for the skinheads, he was at odds with the domesticity around him. He was too wired to relax, too wired to wait for the police to do their job.

He studied Bailey. She wore knee-length jeans, a jade cotton top without sleeves, and sandals. The normalcy made him chomp for action "I'm gonna drive over to Jasper Mini Mart, see if I notice anything new that might help the police with their investigation. An eyewitness view of the scene in daylight might be helpful."

"I'm finished here. Let's go."

In the car, Sam felt a slight knot of anxiety build in the center of his back. He stretched his long body until the joints in his spine cracked in release. Blood thundered against his temples.

Within minutes he stopped his sedan in front of the convenience store. Bailey detected the barely controlled violence within him, a violence that, from seeing the crime scene anew, only escalated. He embodied the fear, the anger, the intolerance felt by their neighborhood. She kept her silence as he adjusted himself to their surroundings.

The heat was dry. Smog clung to their senses, slowing them down so that they too felt heavy. The tainted air stung their eyes, reminding them of just how close they were to the busy expressway used by the skinheads to make their getaway.

Sam switched off his emotions to cast a clinical eye on the view. The convenience store made up the entire left side of the small strip mall, a beige stucco building built on a single level. Starla's Pizza Parlor sat between the convenience store and a real estate office, a leased space with home listings posted in its windows.

A steady flux of foot and car traffic showed that business for the pizza parlor was brisk. Sam noticed that several teenagers stood around gossiping about the hate crime. He heard the words *skinheads, kill, riot.*

His face solemn, Sam scanned the landscaped island near the store. On the island an American flag hung from thick rope. Its blue field of fifty white stars and its thirteen red and white stripes were an emblem of dignity that men of many skin colors fought to faithfully serve and to always protect.

He respected the flag, a symbol of honor he merged with his cultural pride, a pride that swept through him at the patriotic sight. The flag billowed at half mast. A hot breeze made it look majestic and sad, a fitting tribute to Earl's memory.

The flag was dignified and proud, as was Sam when he accepted that racism was dying in America, only slowly, in tiny drops of shared blood. He just wished the blood did not have to be shed from one as young as Earl.

Bailey watched Sam soften when the flag caught his gaze. "It's beautiful, isn't it?"

"Yeah."

"I'm so glad you're okay."

He squeezed her hand. "Come on. Quentin's waving at us to go inside the store."

Even in daylight, Quentin Jasper's store blazed with electric lights, as first Bailey, then Sam walked inside. Advertisements hung from the ceiling on thin silver wire in five eye catching colors: red, blue, green, purple, yellow.

Merchandise packed the store's orderly shelves, each with sturdy brackets made of gray metal. A popular video game arcade filled a corner near the cash register. Until the murder, Jasper Mini Mart was the perfect place to shop for last-minute items.

As Bailey watched, Sam and the store owner shook hands, an act that consummated their mutual dismay at the murder they had witnessed. The men exuded power and pride, the core attributes of living heroes. She admired their vigor.

"It's good to see you," Quentin told Sam. He nodded his head to Bailey, who welcomed the central air that chilled the large store. "How bad are you hurt?"

Sam's lips were drawn into a sharp, grim line, his face hard with fury. "I'm gonna be sore a while, but nothing major, and you?"

Quentin looked him over. "Same. You go to the hospital?"

"No." The few scratches Sam bore were not life threatening.

Quentin squinted at him. "Maybe you should. That's a big knot on the side of your head."

Sam leaned his hip against the service counter, its surface cluttered with chewing gum, key chains, vitamin packs, and condoms. "I'm fine."

Quentin expelled a low breath, then rung up a newspaper for a tall, skinny woman in green plastic curlers. "Good."

Sharp and assessing, Sam eyed Quentin's portly figure.

There was a bruise on his left forearm. "Was it you who called the police yesterday?"

Quentin grimaced. "Yep, didn't do much good though."

Intense emotion throbbed in Sam's voice. "Had they arrived five minutes earlier, they might have caught the skinheads. By the time the police gotta chance to get here, the damage to Earl was done. The boy's name is all over the news."

Quentin sold a six-pack of diet Coke to a stocky man in torn shorts. "Yep, that's what I figger, too. It's a shame. Three armed men against one unarmed man is pretty low. I was happy to find out one of those fools left his baseball bat behind. I bet they're all sweating it out over that little mishap."

Sam shot a quick glance at Bailey, whose support was quiet and constant. "I bet they are, too. I just hope the fingerprints that come up are gonna belong to a man with a police record or something else that'll place his prints on file."

A contemplative look spread over Quentin's face. "Most likely they do have a record of those prints. Those men looked like they knew what they were doing out there. They worked that kid over fast and dirty like they'd done it before."

Sam asked the question that pressed him most. "Did you recognize him?"

"No."

"I thought that since he was on foot he might live nearby."

"Probably, but I'm not here all the time, so it's not a given that I'll recognize everybody who comes through. I feel like I should 'cause I've kept a store in this neighborhood for so long; I've seen many kids around here finish high school. Trouble is, since this area has boomed with new homes and businesses over the last few years, I've lost track of who's who."

Sam stepped aside as a toddler stretched a hand towar
the chewing gum by the cash register. "I saw the way th
skinheads stuck with the kid, even when we stepped in."

Bailey smiled at the toddler's older sister, an attractiv
girl with long, thick braids. The sisters reminded her o
Fern and Sage. "It's almost too sad for words."

Quentin said, "I know what you mean."

"Flying the flag half mast is a great idea," Sam compl
mented.

He respected the older man, especially the way he vo
unteered his time with the youth in their neighborhood
Sam planned to make the same commitment on Monda
by looking into a youth mentorship program.

Quentin tugged his ear. "Least I can do, though som
folks is mad at me for keeping the store open today."

"I wondered if you would," Sam confessed, thinkin
that the hate crime cast a pall over the store's usual friendl
atmosphere. The place had an eerie feel to it.

"Today ain't about business," Quentin explained. "It'
about fellowship. Folks have been coming 'round her
since early this morning to check things out for them
selves. Rubbernecking after the fact is what I call it. Jus
look at those teenagers grumbling out there."

Puzzled, Bailey frowned. "How does keeping the stor
open promote fellowship?"

Quentin's voice expressed the confidence he felt. "I'n
passing out flyers urging folks to keep the peace round
here. I talked to Starla next door. She's opening up he
pizza parlor for a community meeting tomorrow night
We're hoping to get a police officer here to talk to folks
tell 'em they're doing their best to catch those skinheads."

Sam caught hold of Bailey's hand, her steady suppor
much appreciated as he grappled with the hate crime he
had witnessed. "Good idea. It's gonna be a great way to
blow off steam."

Quentin handed three flyers to the boys who had just finished playing on a video game. "Yep, hope it works."

Sam squeezed Bailey's fingers. "It'll work for people who want to rebuild. It might not help the people who want to rip things up to make a point. It happened in Watts during the '60s. It happened again in L.A. during the '90s. It's got a chance of happening this weekend."

Her voice determined, Bailey said, "Sam and I will help you tomorrow, Quentin. I'll see if Ridge Williams is free to speak at the community meeting."

Quentin looked at Sam. "Ain't he the detective that was here last night?"

Sam answered. "Yeah."

"Good man. Young. He talked to me a long while after most everybody else was gone, him and Detective Higgins. Higgins is going to stop by here again today to go over some stuff with me about setting up tomorrow at Starla's. I'm impressed with how Williams and Higgins are busting their butts to keep the peace 'round here. They're good people."

Sam angled his head to the side, a question in his eyes. "I think I've seen that dark blue Thunderbird the skinheads were driving."

"Since last night?" Quentin asked.

"No, I saw it before last night. I just don't remember where."

"Well, you keep thinking on it long enough and the answer will pop up sooner or later."

"Yeah, I've gotta wonder, though, if the skinheads were out to prove some point, or was it some initiation? Earl was a black kid with dark blue eyes. Maybe the skinheads didn't like that about him. Earl stood out."

"What you're saying is that maybe them skins had every intention of doing what they did to that kid? By that I mean you think they didn't just want to beat him up, they wanted to beat him to death?"

"Only the skinheads know the answer to that question."

Quentin's shoulders sagged in dismay. "I wish we had the answer."

Sam released Bailey's hand, scarcely controlled fury in his voice. "I'm gonna find it out." The subtle, pervasive unease in the chilly store escalated a degree.

His stomach clenched, Quentin asked, "How?"

Sam cast his gaze through the glass windows to the American flag. He planned to share the information he and Bailey discovered with the police only. "First, I'm gonna see if I can figure out where I've seen that car before. The model isn't common." Minivans, sedans, and sports cars were popular in their neighborhood.

Thinking furiously, Quentin drummed his fingertips against the counter. "As you said, since the boy was on foot, he probably lives around here. I didn't recognize him, but that ain't unusual. He might have been new to the neighborhood, or he might just come 'round during the daylight hours mostly. I'm here at night usually. Today I'm here because of the killing."

Startled, Sam swung his eyes to Quentin. "You gave me an idea." His brain clicked away at new possibilities.

"What?" Quentin returned Sam's gaze.

"Time of day."

"What about it?"

"I usually stop by here on my way home from work when I want to buy lottery tickets Wednesday nights. It's rare I come around on the weekend because weekends are family time with Bailey and the girls. I probably saw that car on a weeknight."

The idea of skinheads roaming the neighborhood looking for trouble disturbed Bailey. "Do you think they were cruising the neighborhood some night recently and that's when you saw the car?"

"I dunno. Maybe."

Quentin asked, "Have you told the police about seeing the car 'round here?"

"I'm gonna do it today when Ridge stops by later for a witness interview."

Quentin passed out several more flyers to customers. "Good friend of yours?"

"Yeah."

Bailey laid her hand on Sam's forearm. "We all need each other right now. That's why the neighborhood meeting is so special, Quentin. Mind if Sam and I take a few flyers with us to pass around?"

Quentin smiled. "Please do. When these run out, I'll make more."

"We'll see you tomorrow night," she promised. "What time?"

"Six."

Sam grabbed a stack of flyers off the counter. "Bailey and I'll drive around the neighborhood, see if we spot that car."

Quentin grimaced. "Long shot."

Sam eliminated any signs of doubt from his face. "Gotta make it."

Bailey studied the red, black, and green flyers Quentin made for the community. "We'll pass out these while we're at it."

In the sedan with Bailey, Sam watched as a rumbling Camaro classic pulled away from its slot in front of the pizza parlor. A tomcat skirted the creeping juniper beneath the flag pole. Traffic noise from the expressway seemed louder than it had the night before when he had stepped off the same sidewalk, his attention arrested by Earl. The image haunted Sam, as did the premonition of danger.

Ten

While the Walkers talked to Quentin, Digits sat in Snake's apartment, brooding as she listened to him tell Satan's Magic about the race wars. She wished the ceiling would crack open, the falling pieces striking him across his shaved skull; a fitting end for a living monster.

She gripped her cold beer can, her body taut with a red hazed anger. "How can you sit here and tell us that killing someone is okay?"

Snake scarcely blinked, not in the least disturbed by her delayed fit of moral conscience. "It's done. Move on."

"We may all go to jail because we listened to you," Digits said, ashamed of her role in the boot party. "I want out. Today."

Snake stared at each of the four gang members in turn: Holiday, Digits, Bash, and Grip. "Nobody gets out. It's too late."

Holiday fumed, her manicured nails striking a rapid tattoo against her jean-clad thigh. Like everyone else in the room, she wore similar garb to the clothing she had worn to Jasper Mini Mart for the boot party. Their clothing was their trademark.

"Don't even try to think you own us, Snake," she announced. Since Friday, this had become a sore point with her.

His pitiless green eyes glittered in their sockets. He

hated repeating himself. "You were right in there straight from the beginning of last night's episode. You climbed into that car knowing exactly where we were headed, just like everybody else did. You can't get out of this jam, Holiday, because the law won't let you. I won't let you."

"You don't control us," Digits raged, her eyes wild. All they had done was argue over control and responsibility. They lacked both.

"That is exactly why the law won't let you get away with what happened last night," Snake explained slowly, as if she was mentally impaired. "This is the last conversation I plan to have on the subject."

"You're right about one thing," Digits admitted, her eyes downcast, "nobody held a gun to my head. If I wasn't such a coward, I'd turn myself in to my family and to the police. I just never expected for anyone to die last night."

Snake glared at what he considered the weakest links in his gang. "Women!" he scoffed. "You want to ride with us, but you cry when things get a little bit rough."

"You know that isn't true," Digits denied, hating him for being partially right. Like Holiday, she didn't join Satan's Magic to bust heads. She had joined Satan's Magic for companionship, even though the friendship she had found was with those on the fringe of common society. Last night she was a misfit. Today she was an outlaw.

Thinking their little world was about to turn ugly, Holiday downed the cold beer in three bracing gulps. It was early, and all she wanted to do was stay drunk. Instead of simply thinking bad thoughts, she felt mean, scared, fed up with the mess she had made of her young life.

She grabbed another beer off the coffee table, wondering all the while how much crank Bash would consume before he passed out on the dirty apartment floor. He was hyped. They all were.

"I don't even think I can stand this without a drink. I'm going out for more beer," she announced, an awful need to get away from Satan's Magic making her rise unsteadily to her booted feet. The gang was falling apart.

"I ain't letting you go alone. I'm coming with you," Bash decided, thinking fresh air might clear his head. If he was nice enough to her, he thought she might let him ride between her thighs.

Sober, Grip watched Holiday and Bash, and thought perhaps he should go along with them since they were both high. "I'll drive."

"I'll drive myself. Give me the keys, Digits." Holiday demanded. She was tired of domineering men, tired of the lack of control in her life. She needed change, if only briefly.

"You're too wasted to drive," Digits argued, not wanting another death on her mind.

"Two beers do not a souse make," Holiday countered.

Digits glowered at her cocky, off-beat humor. "Very funny."

Holiday's smile was crooked. "I thought so."

Smiling wickedly, Snake looked forward to the upcoming fireworks he anticipated between the skinhead women. It made him horny for sex. "Give her the keys, Digits, then come with me into the bedroom."

Digits spread her fingers into talons. "No."

"No to what?" Snake asked, his voice calm, deadly. He was the image of his namesake.

"No to the blasted keys, Snake. No to *you*, especially to you."

He advanced on her, his face composed. "I see right now how much you need to be mastered. I'm just the man to do it."

She hissed at him, though she never backed away. "Never."

He stopped within an inch of her body, as she trembled with anger. "That word is just the challenge I need to get our little thing started. I didn't get a taste of you last night."

Bash laughed, then grabbed Digits from behind to take the keys from her front pocket. "Guess you ain't going to need these."

Grip did not want anybody to master Digits except himself. "Let her alone."

Snake rotated his neck to see him better. "I've never heard you sound so, so—" he hesitated, selecting the right word, "—vicious," he stated, his body pulsing with old scars, disfigurements gained in previous battles with men over women, over territory. This battle had been a long time in coming.

Instead of screaming her frustration, Digits slumped down on the sofa, every nerve in her body wrapped in knots. She had seen enough bloodshed to last her a lifetime. "Calm down, you blasted idiots," she said to Grip and Snake. "I'm not going anywhere with anybody. Holiday, take the car."

Joining Digits on the sofa, Grip took her hands within his own, squeezing them hard. "Last night sure wasn't your fault." They were all guilty of not thinking ahead, not thinking beyond the moment's chaos.

Digits arched a brow, then snatched her palm away. "Save it."

"Things got out of hand," he continued, ignoring the way Snake kicked a leg on the coffee table with his steel-toed boot. Content to rest beside Digits, content to protect her from Snake, Grip settled on the love seat as close to her as she allowed.

Snake scowled at Grip, whose love for Digits blazed in his eyes. It amazed him that she never acknowledged it. "I won't fight you for her because I need you in Satan's Magic," Snake said. "If we divide ourselves, we all fall."

"And don't you forget it," Holiday warned on her way out of the door, unwilling to tell Bash they were going to drive by the scene of their crime. She wanted to make sure what happened Friday night was not a dream from which there was no escape.

Pulling out of the Jasper Mini Mart parking lot, a flash of blue crossed Sam's vision. "What!" he bellowed as he slammed his foot on the accelerator. His tires squealed.

Alarmed at his reaction, Bailey threw her seat buckle into its slot, her eyes riveted on the single flash of dark blue, an old Thunderbird with a man and a woman in the front seat. "It can't be them," she breathed, knowing it probably was, based on Sam's description.

"It is." The statement was grim.

Bailey's decision was quick. "Get 'em, baby."

He gunned the engine. At the moment he accelerated Holiday spotted his car, then headed for the expressway, Sam right behind her. At last he had some action.

Scared, Holiday was reckless as she tried to get away from him. She had the answer to her question about whether or not she dreamed Earl's murder. She recognized Sam from the boot party Friday night.

"Hold on, Bailey," Sam advised gruffly, his body in tune with her anxiety because he knew her so well. He also knew that her trust in his ability to think straight was being put to a savage test.

Chasing skinheads was risky because neither he nor Bailey were professional sleuths. A man of action, it was hard for Sam to wait for the New Hope Township Police. He was a man on a mission to catch the enemy.

Even though most of his mind was focused on driving, Sam heard the sharp intake of Bailey's breath, saw the way her narrow foot pressed against the carpeted floor of the sedan as if to stop their car from its headlong flight into traffic.

Sam hoped that after all the drama died down, he and

Bailey could resume their married life with the same gusto they had in the past. He knew he should wait for the police, but he was much too close to the answers he wanted about Earl's death. The chase was on.

"They're getting away!" Bailey hollered as she grabbed the leather dashboard to brace herself.

"Not if I can help it," Sam stated. His brows were frazzled in concentration. His big thighs bunched and flexed as they clutched the seat of his speeding sedan. Bailey cheered him on because she too wanted justice for Earl.

A startled male driver flicked Sam a nasty middle finger. He ignored it, saying to Bailey, "I'm gaining on 'em."

Her eyes blazed at her hero. "Go for it, baby. You can do it."

Sam concentrated on Holiday. When she cut from the center lane into the fast lane, avoiding a red Geo Prism, so did he. When she hit the breaks in a curve, Sam kept going. Bailey screamed. Sam rammed Holiday's bumper.

Inside the Thunderbird, Bash cursed until he was red in the face. "Can't you go any faster!" he yelled at Holiday.

"Shut up!" she yelled back, just as Sam rammed her again. Inside the sedan, Bailey clutched the dash so hard her fingernail broke.

"Hold on, Bailey," Sam advised, "I'm gonna force their car off the road onto the shoulder."

Bailey glanced at the field of dry grass. "Let's do it." Sam did. Holiday ran off the road, then righted the car.

Inside the Thunderbird, Bash was furious. "Slow down, Holiday, I'm gonna shoot that dude."

Holiday stepped on the gas. "No."

Bash swore at her when Sam pulled so close to Holiday that she freaked out. The Thunderbird slid along a guard rail; the screeching sound making his skin crawl. He noticed Holiday was shaking.

"Don't flip out," he ordered. "I'm gonna end this thing." Bash whipped out a pistol.

Holiday screamed, "No!"

"Yes." Bash fired two rounds. Sam fishtailed. Bailey screamed.

"We have got to stop, Sam," she told him, her voice tight. He said nothing. She glanced at him. "Sam?" He was oblivious to everything in the world except that dark blue Thunderbird. He was relentless. Bailey backed him up by keeping her mouth shut so he could concentrate.

Bash shot off the Sedan's sideview mirror. Sam rammed the car's bumper. Bailey broke another fingernail.

The Walkers had been in danger together before, but this danger with the skinheads was unnerving, unreal, and utterly compelling. There was no past or future, only the present.

Sam chanced a glance at Bailey, his face commanding. He willed her to trust him, to believe their world would again twirl on its familiar axis, but he knew he would be lying if he told her nothing bad could happen, lying and be damned for it, because he meant to trail those skinheads until the bitter end.

Fascinated with his daring mood, Bailey watched him drive with a swiftness that broke every rule on the car-studded road. He thought only of vengeance for the boy he had held to his chest, held until the act was no longer justified.

Swaying left near the steering wheel, then right near the passenger door with the motion of Sam's car, Bailey knew he would never be the same. Last night he had learned that no day was guaranteed, which was why he was living this moment, and hers, as if it was their last. Suddenly, her mind rebelled at the notion.

"Slow down," she urged, her heart flapping fast in fear, the repeat gunfire a sinister element in the car chase. Disaster was close, too close.

"Trust me," Sam said, driving faster.

Bailey watched in disbelief as the slender, grinning man

n the passenger seat of the Thunderbird once again eaned his torso from his open window, a pistol in his steady hand, sunshine bouncing off his bald head. Gunfire pierced Sam's windshield.

Sam wrapped his palm around Bailey's neck and forced her head down so hard it rammed her brows against the bones of her shaking knees.

"Duck!" he bellowed, shocked at the cracked glass, but not shocked enough to slow his sailing car down even one mile-per-hour. Instead of slowing down he sped up, dodging bullets, avoiding skidding cars as if he was born to drive this crazy.

"You duck!" Bailey wailed, her eyes squeezed so tight her lashes scraped the balls of her eyes. She was almost too scared to pray.

"I can't duck, sugar, I'm driving." He sounded so reasonable, Bailey peeked at him.

She supported him throughout the car chase, but now, with gunfire blasting on the expressway and glass breaking in her lap, she knew it was time to stop. They had to change tactics, capture the skinheads some other way.

Sam felt her eye on him. "They have the answers to my question, Bailey, and the question is, Why? I already know who did it, I just wanna know why." Bailey understood. She had pondered the same question during their first murder mystery.

Another bullet slammed into the sedan. Sam swerved wildly to dodge a Mac truck, loaded down with green tomatoes. Bailey wanted desperately to fling herself to her knees on the floor, but was afraid to snap off her seatbelt in case they crashed. Sam glanced at her, his face intense.

He was grateful that she trusted him. Her trust brought him back to his senses. They had so much to lose and their girls to consider. Sam slowed his pace.

"Damn," he muttered. Dangerous as it was he did not want to quit, even though it was time.

Bailey's heart slammed against her ribs. "That wa
close."

"You okay?"

"Yes." Bailey was proud of Sam. He was using all his wi
and strength to fight a racist hate crime which tore th
edges of his heart and soul. He was a living masterpiec
her masterpiece.

Utterly distracted, almost hungrily, he tracked the Thur
derbird until it squealed out of sight. Dimly, slowly, th
absence of police sirens penetrated his mind. He looke
at the slivers of glass in their laps and shuddered. "Let
take the side streets home."

Bailey breathed a sigh of relief. "Great idea."

The side streets yielded a spectacular discover
"Bailey!" Sam roared. "That's it!"

Fear hammered against her chest. "What's it!"

"The house where I've seen the car!"

Bailey groaned. "This can't be real."

"We've gotta stop."

Bailey squared up. "Go for it."

Sam pulled his car in front of a large contemporar
home. It was yellow with white trim. A Ford Blazer too
up one half of the driveway, Sam's damaged sedan too
up the other half. "Ready?" he asked Bailey.

"Ready." Her brown eyes adored him. It was not ever
day a woman shared an adventure of a lifetime with th
man she loved. Bailey savored all the crazy details of th
jam-packed day.

Side by side they headed toward the front door, whic
opened immediately. "What do you want?" a man de
manded. Of average height, the man was thickly built. H
wore olive slacks, a beige shirt, dark brown shoes an
matching dark brown belt. His eyes were bloodshot, th
expression on his brown face haggard.

Sam stepped forward, feeling an odd sense of déjà vu
"My name is Sam Walker. This is my wife, Bailey. We'v

gotta few questions to ask you about an old Thunderbird I've seen parked in front of this house."

The man froze. "Walker?"

Premonition prickled Sam's spine. "Yeah."

The man spoke with wonder in his voice. "You're the man who helped my son."

Clutching Sam's arm, Bailey gasped.

"Melvin?" a woman in the background queried. "Who are these people?"

The man at the door said, "Donna, you won't believe it, but this is Sam Walker, the man the news reports say helped Earl."

Glad for the opportunity to thank him, Donna Stackhouse offered her hand in greeting to Sam. "Come in. I wondered why you looked a little . . . beat up. Now I know why. Please, come out of the heat."

Ten minutes later Donna sat beside her husband in their traditional-style living room feeling totally upset. She wore a soft cream skirt, cream blouse, cream stockings, cream shoes, gold belt, and gold jewelry as if looking good might lift her spirits. It did not. Like Melvin, she listened to the Walkers in stunned dismay.

Melvin forced himself to relax, to take deep measured breaths, as he studied the Walkers with angry eyes. In Melvin's hand was the sketch of his stepdaughter, Wendy, the sketch Sam had stolen from Grip's apartment. Earl's father was reeling from Sam's description of the past thirty-six hours.

"You're telling me that you saw Wendy at . . . you saw her driving . . ." Melvin threw the sketch at Sam. "No!"

Sam held his ground. "I'm sorry."

Donna jumped to her feet, her blue eyes wild. They were Earl's eyes. "Get out," she demanded. Her voice was hoarse.

Sam folded the artist's pencil sketch, put it in his back pocket, then ushered Bailey to the front door, his hand at the small of her back. Donna and Melvin Stackhouse did not see them out.

After the Walkers departed, Earl's parents sat in their living room wondering how in the world their lives could have become so confused. "Where did we go wrong, Melvin?" Donna asked, her voice hushed as she studied her husband.

Melvin grasped her shoulders, then winced at the purple shadows beneath her sapphire-colored eyes. "We didn't fail our kids, Donna."

She tried to shrug free of his arms, but he would not release her. Slowly, his solid warmth pierced the freezing cold in her bones. "How can you say that when we've lost one child and don't know where the other one is?"

Rage pinched Melvin's cheeks. "We raised those children the best way we knew how. Earl and Wendy weren't abused or neglected. We live in a great neighborhood with great schools. We work hard. At some point, children aren't children anymore. They've got to stand on their own."

Glassy-eyed with disbelief, Donna's slim nose was red from weeping. "Skinheads," she said, her voice an incredulous whisper.

Melvin slammed his fist on the arm of his chair. "Where's Wendy? That sketch looked just like her." A raw anger flicked through Melvin's mind. "She should be home."

"She can't stand being in this house, knowing Earl won't be coming back. I don't blame her. As far as that sketch goes, it can't be Wendy. It just can't."

"We need to ask her what's going on. It's too much of a coincidence that Walker saw a car that looked like hers and carried a drawing of her, a dead-ringer. If we're honest with ourselves, Donna, we'll admit she's involved somehow."

"I can't hardly take it all in," Donna wailed. "Nothing

makes sense. Earl said he would be right back! He would be right back!"

Melvin gathered her close. She was shaking all over with a grief they both shared. "Whatever happens, Donna, we did our best."

"It wasn't enough!"

"Shhh," he whispered, squeezing her tight.

With a long, shuddering breath, Donna let her husband comfort her, let him draw her away from the hysteria that howled around her. In turn, her closeness comforted him. "Oh, Melvin, what are we gonna do?"

"Survive, my love. We will survive."

Meanwhile, Wendy drove listlessly to her destination, aware that she had lost forever the chance to make things right between herself and Earl, lost the chance to tell him how much she loved him. Their last conversation had been an argument at home, on the day he died. The reason for their argument was trivial to her now.

The early afternoon traffic flowed smoothly, on yet another beautiful summer day, a day that weathermen across the state of California said would be the last in the unusual August heat wave; but Wendy failed to notice the smooth, light traffic or the hot weather as she drove to a small neighborhood park located between New Hope and Trinity City.

Feeling a tear leave her eye and trail the length of one cheek, Wendy pulled under a twenty-foot shade tree, a gnarled tree that sheltered a redwood bench near the children's playground. Sitting still in her car, dashing tears away with trembling fingers, she turned her mind to the terrible argument she had shared with Earl on the day he died. . . .

"Earl!" she shouted so loud that her voice shook with the effort, her slender body trembling in a series of muscle spasms. Her fist slammed hard against the deeply grooved panel of his bedroom door closed firmly against her.

"Open up!" she shouted.

Earl shouted back. "Hold on a minute! I'm coming!"

"I'm grounded because of you!" she hollered at him, flinging the words like rough edged pieces of weathered stone. Earl had opened the door. Brisk, powerful strides carried her into Earl's colorful room.

Using the back of her hand and the sweep of her arm, Wendy pushed him roughly to the side, her body strung high, her feelings jumbled with jealous rage. She didn't care as he stumbled into his beloved telescope, the instrument thudding against the rough carpeted floor, its knobby texture at one with the blue curtains and the decorated walls.

"Why did you open your big mouth!" she spat at him.

"Man, you get on my nerves!" With steady hands, Earl righted his steel, gray companion from its side on the blue carpeted floor.

Wendy watched Earl, at ease in his sanctuary, the micro world that was his bedroom, its ceiling covered with stars, bordering all the known planets within the universe. Earl's dreams were like those planets, within the reach of his mind, beyond the grasp of his hand. He planned to be an astronaut someday.

"We went through all this before, anyway," he said. "It's over."

"It's not over, you arrogant son of a—!" Enraged, Wendy slammed her open palm against Earl's left shoulder bone. Crouching low, her muscles taut beneath her jeans, she primed herself to do it again.

Earl fought to stay calm, a hard task for him to achieve just then. He braced himself for more blows as he visibly forced his lean muscles to relax. He breathed softly through his nose, slowly, in and out. Wendy knew he was tempted, but Earl refused to hit her back.

"Fight me back," she challenged him, wanting to bring down their parents' wrath. They had grounded her when Earl had squealed about her late night escapades.

So what if she left their home repeatedly after midnight to catch a ride with friends? Wendy fumed as she stood before Earl. Who cared? Certainly not her parents, who revealed their disappointment in her time and again through solemn, questioning eyes, whenever she broke curfew, whenever she landed herself in trouble somehow.

Earl let his breath out in a whoosh. "No, Wendy. We're too old for this crap. Just get out of my room. Now!"

Flustered by his response, Wendy prowled his book-adorned room, her body rigid as she scanned everything, touching nothing, though she wanted to destroy every little thing in sight. "I hate you."

"So what else is new?"

Wendy's livid face zoomed within an inch of Earl's nose, her hands balled into punishing fists, a rapid pulse beating at her temples. "Shut up!" She snarled the words separately, distinctly.

"If you don't get out now, I'm telling Mom and Dad everything."

"I won't let you."

Annoyed with her childish ways, Earl refused to listen anymore. "You can't stop me."

Incensed, she stepped forward, her youthful body electric with wrath. "I can do a lot of things, Earl."

"So I've heard."

Wendy's temper cracked like liquid oil splashed on a hot iron skillet. Swiftly, she raised her nails to scratch his face. She could never get even with Earl because Earl never lost his temper. Without a word or a fighting gesture, he twirled on his rubber-soled heels and walked away. . . .

At the playground between New Hope and Trinity City, Wendy knew why she did not want to go home and grieve the loss of her brother with her parents. She stayed away

from home because in her most secret, morbid jealousie
she had imagined Earl's death.

As Wendy was leaving the shade of the old tree to mee
her friends, Sam was parking his battered sedan in th
garage while Bailey called the police. "How do you feel?"
he asked, after the patrol officers had gone. He and Baile
were sitting at the table in their breakfast nook.

"Pumped. Shaky. Shocked."

"Me too."

Her eyes roamed the kitchen. It looked clean, brigh
normal. "I'm glad we called the police as soon as we go
home. Do you think they'll find anything useful from th
bullets embedded in your car?"

"Maybe."

"Do you think the skinheads are still in New Hope?"

Sam stopped her roaming gaze with his own. "They'
be crazy to stick around."

Bailey rubbed her temples. "They were crazy to driv
by the store in the first place. Why do you think they di
it?"

"Curious, maybe shocked. You're shaking." Sam ob
served.

"A little."

He caught his breath and held it. "Your teeth are cha
tering."

"Okay, a lot."

Sam stood up from the kitchen table and opened hi
arms. "Come here." She went into them, burying her face
in his strength.

"I love you, Bailey. The way you backed me up today
without question makes me proud. We're good together.'

Her voice was muffled against him. "Maybe too good
If we find ourselves involved in another murder mystery
I'm thinking we ought to quit our day jobs and become
professional gumshoes."

He lifted her chin with his fingers and looked in her

yes. They were soft and warm and beautiful. "I'm glad ou've still got your sense of humor, Watson."

"As you told me once, it's all about perspective, Sherock."

His smile was slow, sensual. "Wanna cook?" he asked, nowing this relaxed her.

"Only if it's in the bedroom."

A trail of clothes marked their progress to their inner anctum. They were old lovers filled with new passion, as he firm palms of Sam's hands cruised the length of Bailey's arms; from shoulder to fingertips they went, then back again.

She swayed against him, as his fingers eased over and down the bones of her shoulders and stretched the length of her arms, wrists, and hands. Down her waist and thighs his fingers went, until she shivered with a pleasure reserved only for him.

Smooth in his seduction, he planted his thighs wide for leverage. In a thrilling, powerful move, he lifted her into his arms so that her calves cupped his waist. With a delicious rush of sensation, she welcomed his body into hers.

Caught up in the luscious moment, she leaned against him, setting them both on fire. She resisted nothing about him; he was completely irresistible. The varied textures of his body grazed her flesh with delight.

He lowered her to the pillows on their bed and applied his tongue to her navel. He left no sensual spot untouched. The wet thrill of his tongue brushed her skin in every place she allowed him access. Dense sounds of satisfaction spilled from Bailey's lips, flowing like dark red wine between them.

"I love you," he confessed to her. Like molten fire his simple declaration touched her in a way that added more flame to the fire of their union. She was a lovely spirit he worshipped in his arms.

After all the suffering since Friday night, he needed to

give, not receive. Bit by glorious bit he worked her over—up and down, back and forth, in and out—so that all she could do was hang on for the hard, sweet ride. Sam was home, deep inside the comfort of Bailey's arms.

A Lunch
between Friends

Spaghetti

Garden Salad

French Bread

Lemonade with Mint Sprigs

Pineapple Sherbet

Eleven

While Sam spent quiet time alone in his basement workshop, where he crafted whirligigs as a hobby, Bailey dialed her girlfriend, Minette Ramsey; hospital administrator at Providence Hospital, New Hope's largest medical facility. "It's true, Minette, we're involved in another murder mystery."

"Good grief, Bailey. You say Ridge is on his way over to discuss the case?"

"Yes, why don't you come over for lunch?" Bailey invited.

"I can't stay for lunch, but I do have some time before a big meeting this afternoon."

"It's Saturday afternoon."

Minette groaned over her heavy workload. "Tell me about it. I'll zip by so we can chat, then I've got to run a few errands."

"Thanks, I could use someone objective to talk to right now. Sam and I are still reeling from the car chase."

Minette heard the tension in Bailey's voice. "I bet you're cooking to relieve the stress."

"Yep."

"What about Sam?" Minette asked, genuinely concerned.

"He's in his workshop, thinking."

The smile on Minette's face came across in her voice. "Designing a new wind machine?"

"Yes, he says it helps him relax. He's also running over everything that's happened in his mind, seeing if he can shake up any more useful clues for Ridge when he gets here today."

"Smart idea," Minette concurred. "I'll see you in about twenty minutes."

"Okay."

As a part-time caterer, Bailey knew her way around the kitchen. For her, making a good meal was like making food for the soul and mind. Wearing a blue sundress splashed with yellow daisies, she went over the lunch menu in her head; spaghetti, french bread, garden salad, pineapple sherbet, and lemonade.

She checked on the spaghetti which she had left to warm. Lifting the silver lid off the emerald green cooking pot, she used a wooden spoon to stir the meat sauce. It was just right. To make the meat sauce, she had used Italian sausage, ground beef, onion, garlic, parsley, basil, oregano, salt, pepper, sugar, tomato paste, crushed tomatoes, water, burgundy wine, and vegetable oil.

She had removed the casing from the sausage with a sharp kitchen knife. She then pulled pieces off each sausage and rolled them into balls. She then put the sausage balls into a large skillet, spread with a thin layer of vegetable oil. She had then covered the skillet with a lid, making sure to open the steam vent near the handle of the lid.

While the sausage balls browned, she had put the ground beef in a separate large skillet. Using a plastic spatula, she broke the meat into small chunks to help the meat brown faster. She did not season the sausage or the ground beef.

While the meat browned, she had chopped the onion up fine, using a Black and Decker Handy Chopper. She put the onion in a big pot. Next, she chopped two large cloves of garlic on her plastic chopping board, shaped like a heart. She added the garlic to the onion in the big pot.

She had measured each seasoning, adding them to the onion and garlic. To this mixture, she added the tomato paste, crushed tomatoes, water, and wine. She stirred the sauce. After the meat browned, she drained off the fat, then added the meat to the sauce.

She had stirred the sauce once more before turning the temperature on the pot to medium. She put the lid on the pot. Once the sauce bubbled hot, she had turned the temperature to low, and simmered the sauce for three hours.

While the sauce had simmered, Bailey cleaned the used dishes and the counter space, creamed her hands with cocoa butter, tossed a fresh tea towel across her left shoulder and set to work on the bread.

She had gathered the six ingredients she needed to make the french bread she planned for lunch: salt, sugar, yeast, flour, yellow cornmeal, egg, oil, and water. Her manicured hands flowed in rhythm with her mind recalling the french bread recipe without need of a cookbook.

She had put part of the flour in a large plastic bowl, added yeast, salt, sugar, oil, and warm water from the stainless steel faucet. She stuck metal blades into the electric hand mixer the girls had presented her with on her birthday. She whipped the fragrant yeast batter with the electric mixer before adding more of the all-purpose flour.

She had unplugged the electric mixer, scraped batter off its blades with a small plastic spatula, set the blades in a sink filled with water, then set the mixer aside until she wiped it down and put it away in the cupboard.

Bailey then added a spoonful of flour to her wooden cutting board, spreading it around with her left palm, dropped the dough onto the cutting board, then started kneading. She kneaded the dough until it was smooth, firm, and dry to the touch.

When she pressed her index finger against the dough, it bounced back. At the sink, she carefully washed batter from between her fingers, then from the underside of her nails. She greased two old cookie sheets with vegetable shortening, then sprinkled them with cornmeal.

After the bread had risen, she shaped the dough into loaves, sliced three thin diagonal lines atop the loaves then covered the loaves with a light dish cloth to let them rise again. She washed her hands, dried them, then spread them with the whipped cocoa butter she kept near the dish liquid along the rim of the kitchen sink. After an hour, she had put the bread in the oven to bake.

Seconds after her arrival, Minette looked at the cool bread and inhaled. "You know I love spending time with you in your kitchen," she said. Sniffing appreciatively, she enjoyed the scent of simmering spaghetti.

Bailey's kitchen was a warm inviting room, where Minette found more than food for her body. She found hope and love, and many wonderful memories to treasure when life turned tragic corners, as it had with Earl's death.

Happy to see Minette once more, Bailey's smooth arms wrapped around her friend's shoulders. Over the years she had learned to celebrate each moment of coming together between the people she cared about most in life.

"I'm glad you came when I called you to tell you about everything that's happened today," she admitted, after their lingering hug and noisy pecks on the cheek.

"Where's Sam?" Minette asked, glancing around.

Bailey's eyes flicked toward the stairwell that led to the subfloor of her large, comfortable home. "He's still in the basement."

"That man and his basement," Minette teased, injecting a smile in her voice. "He's a wizard at those whirligigs he designs. You both are very talented. I find it interesting that he hangs out in his workshop when he's got the blues, while you hang out in the kitchen, your version of a workshop."

A wisp of red-brown hair fell over Bailey's temple as she cocked her head to the side. "I hadn't really thought about it before, but you're right. Even though I've done some cooking today, I'm on pins and needles. I'm glad you stopped by."

Her nutmeg-colored eyes taking in Bailey's earnest face, Minette's mouth curved with affection. "Thanks to you," she said graciously, warmed to know Bailey welcomed her confidence, "I feel comfortable enough here to tell you my trials in life without feeling like a burden. I want you to feel the same way. You've listened to me when I had the blues, about everything from my ex-husband to stress on the job."

"I'm glad I called you. I almost didn't."

"Proud woman," Minette pointed out, as she moved one step behind Bailey, trekking across the oak floor to the kitchen. "Don't you know that in your kitchen, I can relax in peace in the middle of all these flowers you grow so well," she confessed. In Bailey's kitchen, there were yellow hibiscus and purple violets.

Enjoying the distinctive textures of the flowers, Minette ran the tip of one blackberry shaded finger along the decorative blooms of potted plants, their deep vibrant leaves splashed with sunlight, a perfect addition to the country kitchen where her hostess often entertained friends.

Sharing the kitchen with Minette was peaceful for Bailey, too. It showed in the softening of the tiny lines about her mouth and eyes. "If you didn't wait to water your plants until they wilted, your flowers would grow the way mine do."

Minette snorted, a raunchy sound from such an elegant woman, who thrived on board room politics. "Don't you believe it," she urged Bailey as she tossed her leather shoulder bag on the nook table. "What's on your mind?"

Bailey placed a light vegetable snack on the ceramic-tiled center island, her fingers swift and gracious as they performed the familiar task. "This thing with Earl Stackhouse. It has the whole neighborhood in an uproar, especially Sam," she admitted. As a hospital administrator, Bailey thought, Minette knew firsthand how young people inflicted hardship on other people, as the skinhead gang had done to Earl.

Minette's compelling brown eyes scanned her friend's knitted brow, with its wiry strands scattered out of place. "You said he wants to defuse the neighborhood's anger with positive action. What kind of action is he thinking about exactly?"

"Education. Service," Bailey answered, remembering her brief talk with Sam on the way to Quentin's before their incredible car chase.

A shimmer of intrigue slid across Minette's face. Her shoulders lifted, her eyes brightened, and her body leaned forward so that she caught every one of Bailey's softly spoken words. "Like a mentorship program?"

"Yes, he plans to get started on Monday."

"Good idea."

Wondering what she would ever do without the reliable friendship of Minette, Bailey ran one pale palm along the cool surface of the counter beside her. The blue decorator accents on the counter graced the kitchen, by working with the sun to add depth and character to the fragrant space.

Not in the least concerned that Sam might enter the room, Minette kicked off her textured, eel-skin pumps, shoes well coordinated with the fuschia, silk crinkle skirt and matching blouse she wore. With her feet nearly bare, the rough nubs of a blue-and-white checkered rug rubbed against her soles in a tingly way.

Feeling good, she swirled a crisp carrot in Bailey's homemade creamy ranch dressing. Since she adored carrots, she did not doubt that that was the reason Bailey served them. Minette's large teeth made short work of the carrot-nibbling process.

"Even though it's a good idea," she said between crunchy bites, "I think Sam should be careful about working in community business so soon after witnessing such a violent crime."

Bailey's delicate wrists cut through the air, as she waved a carrot in the small space between them. "I think it's a good thing. It beats racing down the expressway chasing bad guys."

Minette tracked Bailey's carrot with her eyes before snagging a fresh one for herself. She had learned during their first murder mystery that the Walkers were risk takers. "Sounds to me as if he's reeling from what happened last night. I can't picture down-to-earth Sam Walker driving hell-bent for leather after a car packed with shooting skinheads. He's hated guns since you were almost killed by one a few years ago."

A teasing gleam in her eye, Bailey pointed at Minette with a carrot tip. "There were only two skinheads, so the car wasn't packed. To tell you the truth, now that we're beyond that little escapade, I admit I was thrilled. Sam was incredible."

Smiling at Bailey, Minette grasped a frosted glass of newly-squeezed lemonade in her hand and took a very satisfying, very long drink. The cold liquid washed away the tiny bits of carrot stuck in her teeth.

Her mouth free to take in more goodies, she reached for another crisp wedge of sweet-tasting carrot. "Even though I've got reservations about Sam jumping headlong into community work so soon after a tragic event, I understand the value of fighting something negative with something positive. Besides, when you two get pumped up, I'd swear you can do anything," she declared, her eyes a strong mixture of loving and laughing.

Bailey gracefully licked a taste of ranch dressing off her finger. She loved homemade ranch dressing, especially the kind they were eating right now, which she had whipped up with herbs from her garden. She had made the dressing Friday morning.

She watched Minette bite her thumbnail in an absent-minded way, as she contemplated slicing more carrots.

Three more carrots would just about finish off the dressing left in the peach-colored crystal bowl.

Minette looked up and laughed. "I'm on a diet."

"I hear you," Bailey urged, while patting her stomach. "The older I get, the harder it is to tell my calories to *burn baby burn.*"

Casting her eyes to the skylight, Minette wagged a finger in Bailey's direction. "Give me a break. With all the cooking you do, I'm shocked to see you keep a size seven on your fanny. Me, I've got hips with a mind all their own. I've got to decline on the extra dressing, especially when I know I've got a business lunch soon."

On the serious side, Bailey's eyes skittered across her executive friend, a comrade who functioned as part sister, part mentor. With Minette's blackberry-toned skin, dark eyes, natural vitality and curvaceous build, she was a sleek woman with a refined, cultured look. She wore her signature fragrance, *Wrappings,* a floral scent.

Bailey thought about Minette's troubled past. "You've really learned how to stick to your guns about what happens in your private life. What I admire most about you is the way you climbed to the top of your profession. You did it with confidence and speed." Minette made a self-deprecating sound.

"I mean it, Minette," Bailey argued. "You've learned how to master your life instead of it being the other way around."

"I went to counseling after my string of terrible relationships. It helped me learn how to live life more fully."

"I admire that, too, about you." In her mind, Bailey believed a woman who lived a full life, on her own terms, was a woman of character.

Pleased with the compliment, Minette's grin split wider than the proverbial Cheshire cat's. "Flattery will get you everywhere with me, good buddy. Feel free to keep it up."

Bailey laughed, a delightful sound in the otherwise quiet

room. Though their tastes in dress were worlds apart, and they did not share the same marital status, they got along great together. "I'm so glad you came. Sure you can't stay for lunch?"

"Positive. As it is, I'm going to have to skip the appetizers at the Rotary Club lunch meeting."

"Ridge will miss seeing you."

Minette's lips curved into a smile. "That Ridge Williams is one fine brother."

Bailey's voice dipped an octave as she leaned forward, mischief in her eyes. "He's single. You're single." She dragged the words out in a sing-song way.

Minette laughed at Bailey's nerve. "Matchmaker."

"Well, how about it? Ridge is a great love candidate."

"Bailey," Minette said in a warning tone.

"I'm serious."

Minette suppressed a smile. "I know, that's what worries me."

"Well, I'd like nothing better than seeing two of my favorite people hook up and have a steamy, loving romance. You're positive you can't stay for lunch? I bet half the people don't show up anyway for that luncheon you're going to later. It's too hot to wear a suit, especially on a Saturday."

"I heard that, but no thank you, even though I'm honestly tempted," Minette answered, her face determined. "In fact, I need to run. I've got to stop by My Girlfriend's Closet to pick up a dress being held for me there." My Girlfriend's Closet was a clothing resale boutique owned by a mutual friend.

Bailey chortled when she pictured Minette's custom-built, walk-in closets, both of them lined with cedar floors. "As if you don't have a ton of clothes to choose from already."

"My only vice. Seriously though, I'm glad you confided in me. There's been times when you saved my life . . . literally," Minette admitted, her voice subdued. Her mind recalled the run-in she had with a murderer, someone Bailey ferreted out for the police. It was also at this time Ridge Williams had entered their lives.

"Boy, was that a mess," Bailey remembered.

"It's also the reason why I can't picture a relationship with Ridge. I associate him with the roughest year in my life. It's the year I admitted to myself I was drawn to men who weren't good for me."

"Ridge is a good man."

"I know. It's just that he's seen me at the lowest point in my life."

Bailey placed a hand over her friend's cool one. "Well, you're fine now. Once you decided to make a change in your behavior, you did. I respect that about you."

"You're the only person I know who can find something good in a lousy situation. I'm glad that time in my life is over."

Scrunching her nose up and lifting her eyes, Bailey tossed Minette a you-can-say-that-again look. "Tell me about it. One of the best things that happened to me and Sam that year was Sage's birth."

"Here, here," Minette saluted, her lemonade held high in the air. "You two make the most adorable children," she admitted wistfully. "That Sage is a riot with all her outspoken ways."

Bailey agreed. "That's just about what Sam's mother told me when I called to check on the girls just before you got here."

Minette's fingers stroked the clean countertop. It was cool and slick beneath her skin. "Lately I've been thinking about a family of my own. I'm ready. Talking about the girls gets me in that state of mind."

"Got any candidates in mind?" Bailey quizzed.

"One."

Bailey's eyes were big. "Are you serious?"

"Very serious."

"But who?"

"Victor Griffin."

"*The* Victor Griffin?" Bailey squealed. The entrepreneur was a hunk.

"The one and only."

"Why, he's perfect, Minette! I didn't know you two were friends."

"We've been quiet about it."

"Why?"

"I'm being careful about our relationship . . . taking things slow."

Bailey leaned a little closer to her friend. "How does he feel about that?"

"Like a tiger in waiting."

Bailey laughed. "I thought Ridge was a great match for you, but that's because I'm crazy about you both, but to tell you the truth, Victor is perfect, a much better match for you."

Minette rolled her eyes. "Uh-oh, I sense those match-making wheels of yours are spinning like crazy. How did we ever get on this subject anyway?"

"The girls. After talking about the murder last night I guess we kind of moved on to something more light-hearted."

"True. Why do you think Victor is perfect?"

Bailey was quick to answer. "He's handsome, strong willed, and socially well connected in New Hope. So are you. You guys are movers and shakers. The more I think about it, you two make a perfect match."

Minette started clearing away the dishes. "Bailey, I'm glad my stopping by helped you feel better, Lord knows you've been there for me, but if I don't get out of here soon I might find myself hearing wedding bells."

Bailey laughed. "Now that's a pretty sound."

Minette laughed with her. "Come on. I want to see Sam before I head out. Talk about a hero. Wow!"

Before heading to the stairwell leading to Sam's work shop, the women hugged each other, in an embrace as warm and cozy as Bailey's kitchen.

Twelve

Ridge's charcoal-colored slacks and dove-gray shirt added to the August heat that burned around him, so close he felt claustrophobic. He arranged his star-witness interviews according to distance, beginning with the farthest witness, Barbara Johnson, and ending with his final witness, Sam Walker. He spoke at length with Quentin Jasper on Friday night.

Ridge knocked on the oak door of his first witness. When the heavy door quickly opened, he stuck a professional smile on his face, then introduced himself. "I'm Detective Ridge Williams of the New Hope Township Police Department. I'm here to see Barbara Johnson."

"We spoke on the phone. Come in," Barbara invited, her dark gray eyes assessing him openly. By the mature sound of his voice over her telephone, she had expected a much older man.

A glance at the handsome detective's left hand proved to Barbara that, like her, he was not married. She wondered if he was ringless but attached to someone, as was the case between herself and her live-in lover, Raoul.

When Ridge removed his dark shades, he saw a petite woman, whom he guessed was in her late forties. She looked good in pale yellow stretch pants, a floral print blouse, and a pair of gold sandals.

"Thank you," he said, responding to her request to en-

ter her air conditioned home. The total quiet in the background suggested to Ridge she was alone.

"May I pour you a lemonade?" she asked as she led him
away from the Spanish-tiled foyer into the living room,
which was wonderfully cool after the heat, which weather
forecasters expected to last until Monday. The detective
longed for autumn.

"Yes, please," he replied, his tone grateful, sincere. His
throat was dry.

"My pleasure," she answered, her voice a purr in her
throat.

Sitting in an easy chair, Ridge studied the lavish living
room while he waited for her to return from the kitchen.
The apartment was meticulously clean, impeccably taste-
ful, echoing the owner's personality. He admired her taste.

A gorgeous view of the foothills showed through cathe-
dral windows along the entire length of the east wall.
Framed Synthia Saint James prints adorned the rest of the
stark white walls, their bold shades an asset to the home's
tropical decor. It was a feminine home, without being frilly.

"Here you are," Barbara said as she placed the cold
glass of lemonade on the heavy wicker end table at his left.
She enjoyed the way he stood up when she approached
his leather chair, as if it was second nature for him to be
a gentleman. She liked this quality in him.

He waited for her to sit on the cream leather sofa opposite him before taking a sip from his frosted glass. "Delicious," he murmured, his tone neutral, polite, at ease.

"Thank you, Detective. Shall we get started?"

"Of course," he replied as he opened his six-by-four-
inch memo pad to a fresh, crisp page. His silver mechanical pencil was set to go. "What did you see, Ms. Johnson?"
he asked, using a professional tone.

"Call me Barbara, won't you?"

"Barbara."

"I heard one of the skinhead women call the other one Holiday," she said to get things started.

Ridge noted the name she gave him on his handy memo pad. "Which woman was identified?"

"The blonde," Barbara answered quickly, as if just thinking about the evening cast a wet cloud over her day. "I was on my way out of the pizza parlor when I saw the fight. I was so scared, I almost dropped my pizza."

"What else did you notice?"

Barbara shuddered. She hated thinking about the crime she had witnessed so unexpectedly. "The blonde's eyes were glazed over, trance-like. I wanted to smack some sense into the woman."

"I'm glad you didn't." The deepness of Ridge's voice added weight to his words.

"So am I," she admitted, her voice weighted with sorrow. "Those boys beat the hell outta that poor kid. Shocked as I was, I didn't want to be the next toy at their boot party, even though I tried to help."

"So you're familiar with skinhead gangs?"

"Being single, I make it a point to know the racial climate where I live," she told him carefully, her words precisely spoken. She was not naive.

Ridge leaned forward slightly, his gaze meeting hers. "Would you know any of the skinheads were you shown photos, or a police lineup? And if so, would you testify against them in a courtroom?"

"The women I'd remember for sure from photos, and yes, I'd testify," she quickly answered.

Ridge lifted a questioning brow at the grimace on Barbara's oval shaped face. Her coral-painted lips were pursed, her hands gripped her plump thighs a little harder. "Why only the women?" he asked, his tone curious.

"The men were in such a frenzy I couldn't make heads or tails of them. Even though the women were vocal, they were also pretty stationary."

"Did you make eye contact with either woman?"

"Yes."

"With which one?"

"Both women. I wanted to figure out, even in a small way, why any woman would urge the public death of someone else."

"What impressions did you get?" Barbara's report was helping him get a feel for the mood of the crime scene before the police arrived.

"Excitement mostly. Also, the girls were in their late teens or early twenties . . . women, in my book."

"In mine, too."

At the sound of keys jangling at the lock on Barbara's door, their conversation stopped abruptly. Ridge tensed on reflex, but stopped short of rising from his seat when he saw that Barbara was at ease, a slight line of worry creasing her forehead. He sensed trouble.

"That'll be Raoul," she explained, wishing she had told her Latin lover about the interview. How could she know that a handsome, sexy, dashing detective would arrive, or that Raoul might leave the gym early for home?

His brows brought together in a frown, Raoul shut the door softly behind him, his mind spinning for a moment around why a man was sipping lemonade in the quiet house across from his shapely, vivacious woman. His body readied for battle.

Dropping his gym bag with a thud, testosterone kicked Raoul's jealousy into full gear. He asked, *"Como estas,* Barbara?"

"I'm fine," she answered, her voice even, though she felt electrified by the turn of events. Raoul used Spanish only when he was angry with her, or when she excited him in the wrought-iron bed they shared. His jealousy turned her on.

A medium-size man, Raoul focused on the stranger in the living room. His body was taut, his feet planted solid on the tiled floor. *"Que pasa?"* he asked Barbara again, though he never shifted his gaze from Ridge.

Barbara spoke fluent Spanish, but she preferred not to play Raoul's rude little game before the detective. Neither she nor Raoul considered Ridge might speak Spanish as well, which he did. He knew Raoul had just asked Barbara, "What's going on?"

"Please speak English for our guest, Raoul," she admonished her angry lover. "This is Detective Ridge Williams of the New Hope Township Police Department."

Raoul spoke quietly, though his eyes were penetrating, his compact body loose in readiness to fight the other man in the room. "Fine. I repeat, 'What's going on?' "

Ridge flipped closed his memo pad, then downed the rest of his cold lemonade before rising from his seat. As he listened, Barbara explained the reason why Ridge sat sipping a drink in the lovely peace of their tropical-hued living room.

When she had concluded, Ridge added, "I appreciate your help, Ms. Johnson. If you think of anything else, please call me." He handed her a business card, an efficient white one with black print.

"I will, Detective," she agreed, smiling. She grazed her fingers briefly against his because she appreciated his switch from Barbara to Ms. Johnson. She was not afraid of Raoul, she simply saw no need to rile him further.

As the twinkling-eyed detective bid his hostess farewell, he bet it would not take long before Barbara and Raoul were sliding between the bed sheets when he saw that the possessive glint in Raoul's eyes was met by the challenge in hers. They had a good thing going.

Outside, Ridge donned his dark sun shades, then headed toward his next crime witness interview. It took thirty minutes to reach once he had pulled away from the tire-scuffed curb at Barbara Johnson's place.

Ridge was hungry and hot when he edged his car against

the curb in front of 2950 Jupiter Way, home to Benjamin
Reilly. His dark shades slid down the bridge of his sweaty nose.
Sweat ran in rivulets down his back as he walked up the cement
porch steps to his prescheduled witness interview.

Before he could knock the door opened, revealing a
gray haired man of sixty-plus years. The man smiled. "You
Detective Williams?" he asked without preamble. The man
was warm, approachable.

Ridge's eyes lit up, glad to meet an upbeat witness. "Yes."

"Well, come on in then. I'm Benjamin Reilly. Call me
Ben."

Ridge shook hands with Ben, then showed proper identification.

"Like some water?" Ben asked, as he led Ridge to the
kitchen table of heavy oak, with clawed feet. The slight
limp in Ben's left leg slowed him down a little, though his
energy level ran high.

"Please."

Ben smiled. "No problem, I been drinkin' gallons myself
while this heat wave is going on."

Sitting in an oak Windsor chair at the polished wood
table, Ridge decided he liked Ben's easy, friendly manner.
From the gleaming copper pots hanging from a cast iron
rack on the ceiling, he saw Ben knew how to handle himself at the kitchen stove.

"Hot as Hades out there ain't it?" Ben queried, to get
things rolling.

"Hotter."

Ben smiled, a move that split his face into myriad wrin-
kles. Sitting in the kitchen table chair opposite Ridge, his
gaze showed how much he liked the younger man. At his
age, Ben seldom wasted time on idle chatter. "You'll find
them skinheads, won't you?"

"I will," Ridge pledged, as he opened his six-by-four-
inch memo pad. The silver mechanical pencil was poised
to write. "What did you see, Ben?"

The older man's expression turned grim. "Murder."

The bond between Ridge and Ben deepened with the solitary word. Each man wanted fast, legal results to avenge Earl's death. "I need details to catch the boy's killers," Ridge stated, his tone subdued, firm.

Ben pulled a sheet of paper from his shirt pocket, almost hidden by the bib of his faded blue coveralls. "That's why I got these notes."

"I'm ready," Ridge told him, not surprised Ben was prepared. Everything about Benjamin Reilly was orderly and efficient. He made an excellent crime witness.

"There were five skinheads. They looked young, but they were prob'ly in their late teens or early twenties. All but one wore T-shirts. I heard names: Grip, Bash, Snake, Digits."

Ridge wrote fast and furious in his notepad. "Did you match body descriptions with names?"

"Only the girl . . . Digits. She's brunette; short, maybe five feet, 105-110 pounds. She had the words Fight ZOG printed on the back of her shirt."

"What do you remember about the other girl?"

"Short, greasy blonde hair, very skinny. A Confederate flag was stitched on the back of her shirt. Her boots had metal toes."

Ridge flipped to another clean page in his notepad. "Anything else?"

"One more thing."

"Yes?"

Ben smiled so wide, Ridge saw clear to his back teeth. "I got the license plate numbers on that old blue Thunderbird. The plate was in the lower left corner of the rear window instead of on either the front or back grill where it belongs. I almost didn't see it because of other junk in the window."

Ridge grinned. This was his first break in the case.

Thirteen

After his interview with Benjamin Reilly, Ridge knocked on the Walker's front door, his slacks sticking to his legs with sweat, his shirt smothering his skin like a velvet cloak. He looked forward to a bit of relaxation after his interview with Sam.

Right away Sam opened the door to his friend. The men clasped hands, their sturdy grasp as solid and respectful as their lasting relationship. It had been five years since they first met over a crisis concerning Bailey.

"Where are the girls?" Ridge asked, thinking how they usually charged him at the Walkers' front door. He enjoyed the ritual.

"The girls are visiting with my parents until Sunday night. According to Mom, they're gonna shop 'til they drop."

Ridge's large dimples formed, as he smiled at the picture his mind conjured up of Sam's mother and daughters on a shopping trip at the local mall. They did it often. "Sounds fun. Your dad's their official chauffeur?"

Sam laughed. "As usual. He swears he's never gonna shop with Mom and the girls again because they stop at nearly every store in the mall, but he always does. I'm pretty sure he likes it as much as they do."

Ridge laughed, too. "Where's Bailey?"

Sam ushered Ridge inside his cool home, closing the

door behind him as a barrier to the August heat. "Putting the last touch on lunch. Come on, let's go downstairs to my workshop. We can talk until she calls us up."

Sam watched Ridge stroll about the masculine space of his workshop, a room where the singular scent of wood dust mingled with the scent of the many paints and varnishes he used to decorate the whirligigs and other wind machines he created.

"The quiet is nice. It's been a long morning."

"Thanks. I come here when I need time alone to think. Bailey does the same thing when she gets the blues, only she does it over tea in the sunroom."

Ridge looked around. The basement was installed with a bank of big rectangular windows that filled the area with natural light. Before the windows was the long metal table where Sam designed his wind machines.

On the left corner of the worktable were small stacks of sandpaper in varied grades. Also, there were tracing paper and drafting pencils to mark master designs onto plywood, the most common craft medium Sam used.

To the table's right, Ridge saw Sam's serious hardware; a straight saw, a scroll saw, bow saw, and coping saw. In this area, Sam also stored rasps and knives for whittling. The overall effect of the basement workshop was very masculine.

"I was glad to see you last night," Sam admitted, once the men had settled in chairs.

"I was shocked to see you," Ridge told him, thinking it an understatement.

When he had arrived at the crime scene, a swarm of spectators had gathered as close to the victim's body as the police allowed them to get without disturbing vital forensic evidence. He had not expected one of those people to be Sam. The shock reminded Ridge of how small the world could be sometimes.

Sam sprawled in his chair, his legs crossed at the ankles,

his arms crossed at the chest. His body language was grave
controlled, focused. "With all those emergency light
flashing, the nosy crowd, and patrol officers, it's a wonde
you got a chance to see me at all. I sat as far away fror
them as I could get without leaving the area."

"Because the police needed you for questioning."

Sam released his arms to stretch his shoulders by rollin
them forward then backward. "Tell me about it. Ther
were blue uniforms everywhere."

"They had to be everywhere in order to keep the grow
ing crowd under control," Ridge explained, glad his cc
workers were professional.

Last night they all knew there was little time to allo
personal feelings into the crime scene. Personal feeling
only hampered an investigation. The late August heat wav
made the task of finding evidence and interrogating wit
nesses hard to do.

"The news says some people wanna riot on skinhea
turf," Sam passed along.

"That's what we hear at the police station. It's the reasor
we're working overtime to solve the case. Because tension
are so high, we are being very careful about the information
we gather. When this thing makes it to the court system, w
don't want any snags coming from our department. The
riot business puts pressure on us, though."

"I don't blame people who wanna make trouble for the
skinheads by finding out where they came from and going
after them," Sam said.

"I don't blame people for wanting justice either, but a
riot won't make things better," Ridge advised, as he ab
sentmindedly straightened the paint brushes Sam kept ir
an old mayonnaise jar.

"I know." Sam turned away from Ridge to gaze out o
the window. The leaves on the oak trees that framed hi
view were healthy, strong, green. He loved the trees in hi

rd. They represented a living legacy of strength and en-
urance.

"Bailey and I went to Quentin's this morning. Looking
the strip mall in daylight was strange."

"How so?" Ridge asked, always interested in Sam's opin-
ons.

"Quentin's sons cleaned the area so well, it doesn't look
ke anything bad had happened there. The only sign of
omething wrong at the minimart is the American flag fly-
g at half mast."

Ridge inclined his head as he listened intently. "I no-
ced the flag on the way over here. It's sad to think some-
ne's life ended so brutally, yet the evidence of that death
so quickly washed away." After the police had carefully
anvassed the area for evidence, and photographed the
ime scene from every possible angle, they had removed
he No Trespass signs.

"The flag flying at half mast ought to give people some-
hing positive to think about. Quentin hopes so."

"I do too," Ridge agreed.

"How have the witness interviews been going?" Sam
sked. He was ready for his official interview. He had a lot
f information to pass on about his own investigation.

"They've done great so far," Ridge explained, taking
ut his memo pad and pencil. "I've got cross references
f confirmed names, a probable meeting place, and a de-
ription of the vehicle and plate number too."

"You've confirmed where they came from?"

"Probably Trinity City."

Sam repeated what he saw the night before, then asked
hen he finished, "are you on the verge of making any
rrests?"

"Carlyle and I are extremely close. It looks like we'll
ave to coordinate with Trinity City police."

The delicate nature of joining two separate police teams
om two separate cities on a volatile crime was not lost

on Sam. The stress lines on the smooth skin of his forehea
indicated his great concern. "Is that gonna be a problem"

"I don't think so."

Sam blew a long, noisy breath through his lips; th
sound incongruous with the controlled way he spoke. "Yo
make it sound so easy."

"Coping with a brutal homicide is never easy. In m
many years as a police officer, I've learned to accept
crime as a completed fact."

A shaft of sunlight cast a gleam over the short waves
Sam's hair, as he tilted his head toward Ridge in questio
"Meaning?"

"I mean the deed is done. That completion is a fact th
living must come to grips with because that single fact ca
never be changed. The trouble with a homicide is that th
living are left to wonder *why* the victim died.

"The answer to that question requires a lot of tedio
work by the police. Resolution of the question *why* com
pletes the cycle that begins when a crime is accepted as
completed fact."

His eyes closed briefly as his mind traveled back in r
cent time, Sam recalled seeing the words, POLICE LIN
DO NOT CROSS on the yellow crime scene tape that co
doned off the area around Earl's body. "Is that how yo
handle murder?"

"Yes."

"You've taken the emotion out of the issue."

"In order to do my job."

As he had the night before, Ridge's presence transmi
ted to Sam a deep, fraternal affection. "Has anything els
come to mind about what you witnessed, anything new?

Sam had waited for this moment. He explained ever
thing to his friend, including his breaking and enterin
Ridge listened without interrupting, taking notes on occa
sion. When Sam finished, Ridge leaned forward in his sea

"The skinheads' return to the crime scene was either very bold or very stupid."

"I agree," Sam said.

"You and Bailey alright?"

"Yeah, I'm surprised you haven't heard all about the car. It's pretty messed up."

"Carlyle and I are working closely together. Most likely the report filtered to him because I've been out interviewing witnesses. We're meeting at four o'clock to update each other on the investigation."

"Sounds like you've got it under control."

"As much as possible. Everybody on the case is working tight to solve this crime fast. Did you get the license plate number?" Ridge wanted to have as much corroborating evidence as possible so that he could cross reference facts with Carlyle.

"Bailey got a partial. I've written it down for you." Sam handed Ridge a large index card.

"Good, this matches the number Ben Reilly gave me today. He was the older man who fought at the crime scene."

Sam watched Ridge put the index card in his pocket, the same pocket he used to store his mechanical pencil and his memo pad. "I figured out today why I didn't spot the license plate. It wasn't on the front grill which faced the attack. After the attack, I only thought about Earl. I figured Quentin, the woman with the pizza, or the old man would get the license off the back."

"The license was in the back window, not the back grill."

"That's what Bailey said. I'm surprised I didn't see it the second time. I guess all I could see were the skinheads."

"Although I'm alarmed by the car chase and the breaking and entering, you guys handled yourselves well," Ridge admitted.

"Bailey stuck with the details of the car while I stuck with the driving. The chase was wild."

"Dangerous."

"Unforgettable."

Ridge laughed a little. "I feel like this is a repeat of the first time I met you and Bailey."

"Say what?"

"The last time you and Bailey got into something sticky like this, I told you that you were fortunate you weren't hurt."

"I remember."

Ridge studied his friend. "You're a grown man, so I can't stop you from doing what you feel is right. Just be careful."

Sam was solemn. "I hear you. Why do you think they were at the strip mall today? It was risky."

"Who knows? Maybe they feel guilty, maybe they get a thrill being so close to the scene of their crime. I'll ask them when I see them."

Using two long fingers to stroke his chin, Sam asked, "It should be soon since the skinheads are still in the area."

"That's what I think."

Sam was silent a moment. "I don't understand this riot business really. I understand wanting to get the skinheads by force if needed, but not a full scale riot that's gonna do more harm than good."

"Like you, people are pissed off."

Sam's eyes swung to the windmill whirligig he had left near the window to dry Thursday night. "Yeah."

Ridge closed his much-valued memo pad, retracted the lead in his silver mechanical pencil, then stood up. "Let's head for lunch. I'm starving."

"I know."

"How?"

Sam grinned. "I hear your stomach growling."

In the Walkers' kitchen, the dishwasher hummed and swished, evidence that Ridge and Sam had helped Bailey clear the fragrant room of their late lunch debris. The spaghetti lunch was excellent.

Ridge had enjoyed the sumptuous, feel-good meal Bailey had prepared for them. "Come here, you wonderful woman," he cajoled, his eyes filled with delight.

"One wonderful woman coming up," she teased in return, thankful he liked the meal she and Sam had shared with him. Her only disappointment was that Minette had been unable to stay.

Still holding her loosely in his arms, Ridge looked at Sam over the top of her rose scented, red-brown hair.

"You're a lucky man, my friend," he told Sam after he released Bailey.

"Hey, why do you think I married her?" Sam teased, as he led the way to the den.

In the back part of the century-old farmhouse everything was quiet, so quiet they could hear several birds chirping outside in Bailey's garden. The sounds of nature comforted Sam. The setting was earthy, healing.

Ridge winked at him. "I bet you married her for her decorating skills. Every time I come into this room I want to kick my shoes off."

Sam looked around with fresh eyes. The furniture in the cheerful, child-friendly den was a hodge-podge of colors and comfortable styles. Red-and-white checkered fabric covered the sofa where he sat.

The long sofa's matching armchairs were big, comfortable cream-colored seats with huge splashes of green leaves, yellow flowers, and red flower buds printed across the durable fabric.

Italian majolica, ceramic dishes patterned after vegetables, sat on a huge, weathered buffet and its matching hutch. The television and stereo were black. Boston fern filled the cobblestone fireplace.

Bailey laughed. "Go for it. *Mi casa es su casa,*" she teased in Spanish, "My house is your house."

"After that terrific lunch I'm tempted, but it's time to get to work again. Carlyle and I are doing everything we can to solve this case within forty-eight hours. By Sunday night, we hope to have that skinhead gang locked up in the city jail."

Comforted by the virile presence of two fine males, Bailey explored a possible reason for the beating that led to Earl's death. "Do you think the heat wave prompted the boot party last night?"

"Maybe, I've learned that most crimes committed by young people happen in late summer. August is right before school starts, a time when many people take vacation."

Sam's fists clenched in a quiet, telling gesture of anger. "Are you saying that youth crime is higher at this time of the year because young people have more spare time on their hands?"

"Yes, because people are outside more in the summer, they make easy crime targets, especially thrill crimes. In warm weather months, it isn't uncommon to find a rise in arson, rape, or assault."

"Plus murder," Sam added, a nearly overwhelming sense of anger penetrating his mind.

"Murder and burglary happen most in winter."

Bailey shuddered. "I've always felt safe in New Hope."

At her remark, Ridge strengthened his private vow to see that justice was served to the skinheads. Watching her shudder, he acknowledged his personal, intense hatred that such a warm, lovable woman was uneasy in her own home.

"For the most part," he said, "crime is lower here than it is in larger cities. The greater the population, the greater the crime risk."

"I'm scared." Bailey's confession surprised neither man.

Ridge's voice was solemn. "A little fear is a good thing if it keeps you wary."

Bailey tapped a forefinger against her thigh. Her expression was one of sheer, down-to-earth beauty, unmarred by guile. "I can't believe a neo-Nazi gang attacked someone in New Hope."

Sam leaned forward, the bones of his elbows on the broad caps of his knees. "If neo-Nazi gangs are gutsy enough to come to a fairly small town like New Hope, then what happened last night has got a big chance of happening anywhere."

"This bothers me also," Bailey admitted. "The skinheads took a huge risk coming into this neighborhood on a Friday night. Either they were being very bold, which might stem from confidence in a long battle history together, or they were being amateurish, which might explain why Earl was killed instead of just roughed up. Maybe they lost control."

Sam said, "The quick way they came into this neighborhood and left it goes with either theory. The speed of the crime doesn't seem to be a helpful clue."

"True," Ridge agreed.

Sam continued. "If they were pros, they knew they needed to leave quickly, or the neighborhood might have time to rally and retaliate on Earl's behalf. Such an attack would put the skinheads at a disadvantage. The quick way they came and left the minimart added to the drama of what they did, just like it added to the surprise."

Bailey shivered, unable to keep the conversation at an emotional distance. The night before, she had nearly lost her husband in a battle with strangers over the fate of a young man she would never know. She felt cold.

"But what motivates them to kill?" she asked.

"A soldier's mentality," Sam told her "When it gets down to the wire, soldiers are weapons of war."

"He's right," Ridge confirmed. "The violent skinheads I've met think it's their job to purge our country of people they don't feel belong in it. While not every skinhead is violent, the ones that are violent are weapons in an underworld where white skin rules. Skinheads join gangs for five core reasons anyone joins a gang; survival, family, attention, strength, and respect."

Bailey grimaced. "You're talking about the Ku Klux Klan."

Ridge met her gaze. "Marginally, racist skinheads are a young, weak version of the KKK, an old supremacist group that mixes well in the general public. The skinhead subculture, ruled by young people, works in a blatant way, meaning that you can see them coming a whole lot easier than you can see some people in the Klan."

Sam connected their talk to the ugly events of the night before. "I don't think I'm ever gonna forget Earl's killers. The buzzed hair, thick boots, and clothes make a tough image."

"That's the purpose of the look," Ridge stated. "The common factor between the old and young white supremacist subcultures is the source of their power. In supremacist circles, power comes from being white."

"I'm gonna use the community meeting tomorrow to tell people everything we know about skinheads," Sam stated. "The last thing I want is for more of them to come into New Hope thinking their actions won't go unchallenged."

Bailey liked his strategy. "Great idea."

Sam smiled at her. "Ridge, one of the girls last night wore the words Fight ZOG on her shirt. What does ZOG mean?"

"In white supremacist circles, ZOG is a mythical, Jewish-controlled government called the Zionist Occupational Government."

Bailey shook her head in growing disbelief. "I can't believe we're breaking into the twenty-first century with racial bigotry still an issue. We need to work on poverty, cancer,

AIDS, the nation's deficit, but instead, we're hung up on race."

Sam conceded her point. "This neighborhood meeting sounds better and better."

Ridge agreed. "At least it's a start. At the police department, Earl's death has brought up similar discussions to the one we're having. It's something positive."

"Where are you headed next?" Sam asked.

"The police station. I'm meeting with Carlyle within the hour to review the case. I also want to see what forensics has on the bullets from your car. You also need to call your insurance company."

"Still think you're gonna have the skinheads by Sunday night?" Bailey asked.

"Yes."

Sam said, "I'll do what I can to help."

The men looked at each other a long time before they shook hands. "Be safe," Ridge warned.

Sam answered, "Yeah."

Fourteen

Later that day, harsh music blared from big amplifiers planted around a dark, stifling nightclub in Trinity City. Minorities made up less than five percent of the small city's population. It was 9:00 P.M.

Psychedelic strobe lights whirled across the domed ceiling inside Club X adding mystique to the hot August night. For Snake, Club X was the epitome of a living hell where misery, anger, and resentment found expression in hard-hitting skinhead music.

The music burned away the kind of normal thinking, which would encourage right actions over wrong. Bodies sweat to the thundering beat; tough, young bodies ripe for war. People screamed their excitement, a sound only dimly masked by the driving skinhead beat.

His expression stony, Snake scanned Club X in search of Holiday and Digits, his sexual party favors for the new recruits he wanted to welcome into Satan's Magic; his small, but growing band of society misfits. Like any loving father, he was proud of his creation.

Rubbing his sweaty palms together, Snake looked forward to the orgy he planned later in his tiny one bedroom apartment. A shift in the rough, orgasmic music set his foot tapping with anticipation. The rough music and the hard bodies muffled the sound of his steel-toed boots.

The heavily tattooed disc jockey played the old racist

songs still favored by Snake and his peers; *Reich 'n' Roll*, *The New Storm Troopers*, *Fists of Steel*, *Heads Kicked In*. Snake's heart slammed against his chest to the beat of the fast driving, frenzied music. He seldom danced, preferring to watch people instead. Club X people fascinated him.

Snake liked this nightclub that catered to hard core racist skinheads like himself, men committed to fighting ZOG. Snake believed a zionist would do anything to better Israel, including controlling the American people through business and government. The Zionist Occupational Government was not Snake's idea of utopia.

For him, the perfect utopia would be a dream island, where citizens and government were of a pure white race. Club X was filled with solid specimens of racial purity. Feeling good, feeling proud, Snake's shoulders rocked to the electric music provided in the club.

His slim torso against the nightclub wall, his green eyes shuttered by thick lashes, Snake thought about the color black, his top lip shifting into a slight sneer. He never thought anything black was good. In history, black death was the bubonic plague. To be blackballed was to get negative political votes. A black eye meant a bad reputation.

Blackguards were scoundrels. In movie classics, black maria's were trucks used to carry police prisoners. Black marks meant failure. Black sheep disgraced their family. Black market meant illegal trade.

The only thing good Snake thought of at all that was black was crude oil, something he had heard called black gold, and that phrase had a fancy, rich, light-colored word to it to make his saying it worthwhile.

In contrast to black, Snake saw white as the only pure color in the color spectrum; that color would not absorb other light rays. White flags meant truce. The term *white-haired boy* meant favorite person. White lies were the most harmless lies to tell.

White heat burned metal white. In the dictionary, white

heat defined intense activity and intense emotion. Snake
felt lots of intense emotion about white skin. It was all he
owned, when stripped to nothing.

He had to justify the power of his skin color which was
why he boned up on Klan phrases and rituals. Snake gladly
shared what he learned with Satan's Magic, in a studied
attempt to unify their minds with his private mission.

His private mission in life was to make Satan's Magic a
Klanton, a chapter of the Ku Klux Klan. Once in the Klan,
Snake aspired to gain the title of Exalted Cyclops, the head
of a Klanton. He might reach his goal, as long as the police
didn't catch him for the murder of Earl Stackhouse.

He felt no remorse for the murder because he was almost ready to join the Klan, almost ready to fully embrace
the concept that Nazi's rule and that Hitler lives. First he
wanted to prove himself worthy of the greater cause of
single race domination, hence his fledgling organization,
Satan's Magic.

It was no accident Snake pushed Satan's Magic into the
boot party, which had changed their lives from the moment it began. For his plan to fight a race war he needed
doers, not thinkers or dreamers or people disloyal to him
on a core level. Satan's Magic needed more good, racist
men, men like Bash and Grip; loyal men, corrupt men.

Like-minded racist men flocked to Club X, the meeting
place where Snake found ready candidates for Satan's
Magic, candidates that ranged from the "wannabes" to the
"hard core" skins.

Tonight he singled out the fence straddlers, those people who shifted between being racist skins and anti-racist
skins factions. In his experience, racist skins were violent
while anti-racist skins were not. He wanted men of action.

Oblivious to every other man or woman in the hot,
music-driven club, Snake walked up to Tommy Gun, a
bald man under twenty-five who wore camouflage pants,
an army green T-shirt, and boots.

Tommy Gun was weapons trained by the United States National Guard. Snake coveted Tommy Gun's weapons knowledge, his stockpile of arms, his stash of ammunition. He would make a fine addition to Satan's Magic.

Snake and Tommy Gun conversed near the crescent-shaped bar packed with carousing men and loose women. Pale, sweating bodies gyrated all around them on a scuffed wood floor in violent dance called slam dance. The zealous dance spoke to Snake of race war, his favorite topic.

In his youth, he had learned all about the ins and outs of running a band of men and women, skilled in guerrilla warfare tactics. At the strong sides of his father and uncles, he went to barbecues at secluded campsites to study the business of paramilitary training, the business of specialized hate strategy.

He learned how to build and use small detonation gadgets, how to shoot straight, how to get fake identification if he needed it for himself or for one of his followers, how to pick and recruit a flock. The skills he had learned growing up beneath the wing of warped patriarchs he had used to start Satan's Magic.

For race war, Snake had his eye on two recruits; the weapons specialist Tommy Gun, and the fence straddler known as Head Doctor, an army-trained soldier. Head Doctor was twenty-three, short, stocky, and dressed tonight in a navy muscle shirt, navy jeans, and scuffed basketball shoes.

Snake wanted Head Doctor to carry Satan's Magic beyond the simple gang trade of baseball bats, chains, pipes, table legs, and police batons. Snake coveted Head Doctor's physical fighting skill, his alliances with other neo-Nazi groups.

Snake craved the expertise Head Doctor and Tommy Gun held as military trained soldiers. Through these two new recruits he could access bigger, better war power, power that included assault weapons, combat skills, and the means to sharpen his greatest single weapon of all organized hate.

Snake wanted to do everything within his power to help his brothers reach the Aryan Christian paradise he had heard so much about in his youth. He learned from his father, his uncles, and the leaders of the clandestine Aryan boot camps that it took all kinds of armies to win the number-one spot in the race hierarchy.

The two-year stint he had spent living in underground bomb shelters with his father had enforced in him the belief system that the resistance needed many types of freedom fighters. They needed fighters to combat the federal agents, politicians, lawyers, media, and financial institutions that did not support the Aryan aim to destroy the United States government.

Earl Stackhouse was the taste of blood Snake believed Satan's Magic had needed to push them into the next stage of his vision, a special army of soldiers under his command. He wanted an army that bought into racist rhetoric, which said Adolf Hitler had the right idea when he set about creating a new state, purified of non-Aryan people. For Snake, Club X was potentially a mini Third Reich.

Surging with pride, Snake searched for his growing army of neo-Nazis. He felt strong with purpose, and blessed with leadership skills. Electrified, he wanted sex with Holiday before he passed her around. He moved away from the wall to find her.

Holiday cleared a path to the restroom, dodging Snake when she saw him move away from the wall in her direction. He had told her there were three things you could not give a black person: a black eye, a fat lip, or a good job. At first she had thought it was cute but she had discovered on Friday night that he was wrong.

From the tail of her left eye Holiday saw Bash doing the same thing she was doing: thinking. Of course their reaction was much too late. They were wanted felons.

Sitting alone in a booth sticky with spilled liquor, Bash enjoyed the last of the methamphetamine he had just purchased. No matter how much crank he used, he never was able to recapture the euphoria of his first high. Still, he kept trying.

Sitting by himself in the booth, his body was electric with false energy, his mind was crisply alert, and his emotions were deeply excited. He cared little that Earl Stackhouse was dead. He refused to brood over stuff that couldn't be changed.

Seconds later, Bash left the booth for the dance floor. The roaring, pounding, thrusting music plowed his body as he danced. Delirious, he slammed his body against other hard bodies, his feelings running naked as he bounced on the Club X dance floor. He punched shoulders, rammed chests, threw wild punches into the dense press of revelers who jostled him.

Ignoring the true fights going on in his face, Bash sunk himself inside the pelting music that stretched beyond heavy metal, stretched beyond anything that ever came on the local radio. He was bursting passion, scorching flame, straight energy, pulsing flesh. He loved to slam dance.

The dance made him hunger for sex, which made him hunger for Digits. She claimed she never wanted him, and said things to him during sex that singed the hair off his ears.

He loved this wild streak in her, the wild streak that made her claw his butt during the final throes of her passion. What he did not like was sharing her with Snake's new recruits for the night. He wanted her first, the reason he needed to find her. He sought her out.

Aware Bash would look for her soon, as he always did just before they left Club X, Digits followed Holiday to the restroom. Music thundered from amplifiers, pounding her head. She did not simply trail Holiday to escape Bash's hungry eyes, she trailed Holiday to escape a spokeswoman for Christian Identity, a racist religious group.

Digits stared at herself in the restroom mirror. She wore a green tank top, stonewashed jeans, and low top sneakers. Her eyes were bloodshot. Her hair was greasy. She did not want to hear the religious woman's doctrine that Jews were Satan's children, or that anybody who was not born white was an error God made when he created the world. She could not deal with that warped racist logic tonight. She no longer believed in it.

Cold sober, wearing faded jeans below a ripped cotton T-shirt, Grip's eyes tracked Digits to the restroom from his position near the exit. Grip shifted his eyes from the women's restroom to Snake, who prowled Club X in search of Holiday and Digits.

Grip knew Snake wanted the women to screw the common sense out of his glassy-eyed new recruits, Tommy Gun and Head Hunter. Sex, drugs, fiery rhetoric, and charisma were Snake's weapons in the gang trade; but not for long, Grip vowed, on his way to the public pay phone outside, not with Digits.

Fifteen

Meanwhile, parked in the shadows outside Club X, Sam sat with Bailey in her burgundy Previa minivan. It was dark outside, and there was no movement in the parking lot. The absence of loiterers worked to the Walkers' advantage.

"This feels weird," Bailey muttered half to herself, every hair on her body standing on end; even her goose bumps had goose bumps.

"Wanna go home?"

Bailey felt safe with Sam beside her. She knew he would allow no harm to come her way. "No, but tell me your plan again."

"Watch the people coming out of the nightclub. See if I recognize anybody from last night."

She gathered her breath, held it, then let her breath go in a loud rush. He had once played devil's advocate for her, she did it now for him. "Because this is an official police matter, maybe Ridge or Carlyle should be here with us."

"Ridge and Carlyle don't have jurisdiction in Trinity City. This means that as amateur detectives, we can do a lot of things they can't do because they have to follow police procedure."

She chewed this strategy over. It made sense. "I never thought about what we're doing in that way."

"When Mary Lou Booker died, all you wanted to know

was the truth behind her death. You wanted to understand why she died because something about her death bothered you."

An image of the friend she still missed came to mind. Mary Lou showed Bailey that good friends were often more complex than they appeared on the surface. "I remember."

"Well, I feel the same way about Earl Stackhouse. Not only that, I want to avenge his death by bringing his killers to justice, whether it means working with the police or parallel to the police. Justice has gotta be served, Bailey. I won't rest until it is."

His compassion moved her. Sam was not a man who procrastinated when he believed there was a job to be done. She admired his ability to stay focused on a problem until the problem was solved.

"I'm with you," she told him. "It's just that I don't want to keep anything from you about how I feel, good or bad."

"Thanks for being honest. It's natural to worry a little because we don't know what's gonna happen next."

The silence between them was short-lived. Bailey's stomach yowled as if it held a tiger by the chain. "God! I'm hungry."

He shot her an amused look. "You're the only woman I know who could think of food at a time like this."

His chuckle did marvelous things to her body; it strummed everywhere. "I guess it's nerves. I just can't believe we're on surveillance. I mean, it's all so unreal. I'm scared and excited at the same time."

"One thing I learned from you is that people have gotta follow their instincts. My instincts tell me this is the place to be tonight. I feel it."

Bailey reviewed the last twenty-four hours in her mind. It was late August. There was a heat wave. It was the weekend. A young man was murdered in cold blood. The intense heat, the short time, and the terrible murder created a hot sensation. It had to peak soon.

"What's your action plan?" she asked.

"Play it by ear. Use the camera we brought with us to take pictures of anybody we think are suspects."

Her body tingling with adrenaline, Bailey let loose a surprise confession. "I know this is crazy, but . . . I'm horny as hell!" His laugh gave her butterflies.

"Instead of telling me how unsafe what we're doing is, you're telling me you're not only hungry, but horny, too. You're too much," Sam said.

His bold black gaze commanded her attention, as he stamped his invisible claim over her heart and soul. He was every inch a man, her man. She said, "I'm serious."

The look in his deep black eyes was roguish. "It's gotta be the excitement of the chase."

She negated the idea immediately. He was a hard-working man at his most elemental; inspired, proud, daring, and fearless. "That's probably part of it, but most of it is you."

"How?"

"You've been so charged since Friday night you've become a familiar stranger."

"Say what?"

"Our life is good, but it's an ordinary life because we're ordinary people. I mean, our marriage is comfortable. It's just that since last night, everything about you is . . . dashing."

One bushy brow lifted a bit. "Dashing?"

"Yes, but the best thing in the world about it is that you're all mine!" Her eyes blazed with renewed awareness and sparkling kinship. This man was her soul mate, her lover and friend for life. She felt superb and it showed.

"Come here, woman," he beckoned, the tone husky and deep.

His heavy palm wrapped around her neck, pulling her close, so close his breath mingled with her breath; so close his lips grazed her lips, his tongue tangling with her tongue. He kissed her as if every one of his dreams had come true in that instant. His kiss—dark, mysterious, and compelling—swept her breath away.

Bailey forgot all about surveillance. She was alone with the man she loved, the man who made her feel safe and treasured, the man who defended strangers and protected the innocent. Instead of telling her to stay home, he welcomed her body and mind into the drama that had shattered their weekend. She would climb mountains with him.

Clasping her face with both hands, his stimulating kiss grew deeper. Fire met fire until the flames burst so high the couple broke apart with a gasp. "Now *this* is crazy," he said, remembering where they were and what they had to do.

This time, it was Bailey who laughed. Despite the many years of their marriage, they still shared a heat and a passion able to stop time in its tracks. Her entire body glowed with an incredible, tingling joy.

Ten minutes later, Sam bolted upright, slamming his fist against the steering wheel. "It's him!"

Panic seized Bailey. "Him who?"

"The guy at the pay phone." It was Grip.

Bailey watched Sam set the flash on their instant Polaroid camera. He left the car for a better shot. "Be careful," she warned, her stomach clenched tight. Sam aimed the camera at the skinhead, then snapped his picture.

Grip never noticed the flash, but someone else did. It was Head Hunter. "Hey!" the skinhead called.

Not realizing the danger, accustomed to the noise of the parking lot, Grip leaned into the pay phone, one hand holding the phone to his ear, the other hand pressing against the other ear to block out the shouting.

Bailey saw everything in slow motion, afraid their good luck might run out, caught in enemy territory. "Hurry, Sam! Hurry!" It was too late. Head Hunter was after him.

Just as Sam was about to jump inside the minivan with

Bailey behind the wheel, Head Hunter chucked a rock at the windshield. Sam tossed the camera in the minivan, reversed his steps and faced his pursuer with all the rage he felt over Earl's death. Bailey cut the lights on the minivan to detract attention from the warring men.

"You've got nerve coming to this part of town," the skinhead said. His legs were spread apart, his hands fisted at his sides. He had a small silver ring in his nose.

Sam sized the younger man up, figuring he had at least fifteen pounds on him. "Free country."

"Ain't nothing free."

The skinhead swung his left fist at Sam who blocked it with his right forearm. Quickly, the skinhead anchored his right foot on the ground before aiming a sharp kick at Sam's kneecap. Sam grabbed the skinhead's foot and yanked, knocking the man off balance.

The skinhead came off the ground in a crouch. He tried to tackle Sam, but Sam side-stepped the fighting move, doubled his fists and cracked the skinhead on the back of the neck. Head Hunter went down, but not for long. He came up swinging.

Sam countered this quickness with muscle. He slammed Head Hunter against the minivan. The skinhead hammered his fists against Sam's back to break the hold. Sam released Head Hunter, stepped back and hit him with a quick rhythm of punches; one-two, one-two.

"Hey! What's going on!" They had been spotted by Tommy Gun.

Bailey flicked on the headlights. "Sam! Trouble!" She revved the engine.

In less than a second, Sam coldcocked the skinhead, then jumped into the family van, out of place in the deadly atmosphere. Bailey took off before the passenger door closed, tires squealing, skinheads chasing the car. She outdistanced them in a flash.

"Faster!" Sam bellowed, wanting to get away before the

skinheads regrouped for a car chase. He had no real desire to join another one so soon. Bailey gunned it. Flowering bushes scraped the passenger-side door as she dodged a speed bump. Gravel spun off the rear tires.

Sam slammed his seatbelt into place. "Soon as it's clear, pull over. We gotta call the police before they leave the nightclub."

She risked a glance at him, her heart pounding fierce in her chest. "You all right?"

"Yeah."

She saw a light trickle of blood. "You're cut."

"And my knuckles are swelling, but for now I'm on top of the world. We got 'em, Bailey. We got 'em." She slapped him a high five.

"After we call the police, let's go home."

Visions of steaming spaghetti sauce and moist garlic bread made Bailey's stomach rumble. "Good, I'm starving."

Exhilarated by their safe escape, and by the satisfying clash with Head Hunter, Sam laughed, the sound victorious. "You're incredible."

In two words and a glance, he had singed her fear into ashes, which blew like dust in the wind. "What I am is hungry and horny," she teased, her eyes and tone full of sass.

"I'll see what I can do about that, hot stuff."

She looked at his swelling hands and the slight cut on his face near the left eye. The euphoria of their success had put his pain on hold. Sam was roughed up a bit, but otherwise fine. Her eyes gleamed with mischief. "Are you sure you're up to it, partner?"

"I'm like the pizza man, baby. I always deliver."

Bailey stepped on the gas.

At home in their bedroom, clothes were shucked in a hurry. Hot and gritty, they stepped into the shower, welcoming the water that gushed over them. After their adventures of the day, they needed to reinforce their bond with each other. Only after this revival of the senses was complete would they remember again their pursuit of the skinheads.

His mind as aroused as his body, Sam rediscovered the woman he loved. Her graceful hands worked their magic, as she soaped the skin of his back with a soothing shower sponge scented like spring.

In turn, his touch radiated over Bailey, drawing her ever deeper into the circle of his aura. Her own body slick with water and beads of soap, she nestled against him, as he unveiled the many layers of his love for her through his touch, his spirit, and his mind.

Using his body, Sam celebrated the physical ways he was different from Bailey. He serenaded her with his gaze, telling her in the secret look only lovers know that he cherished her more than any words could express.

Bailey savored his body English. His soapy fingers caressed her back until she purred. His wet thighs brushed her hips so that she purred even more. Her lush sounds of pleasure spurred him to explore far more sacred territory. He rinsed the soap from their bodies, turned off the shower, and stepped onto the rug, drawing her beside him.

Removing the towel from her hair, he pushed his fingers through the thick tresses, pushed them through until they cupped the base of her head. Pliant in his hands, she welcomed his kiss, the kind of kiss only this man, her husband, could give.

Sam was fierce, but never hurtful. He kneaded and caressed her body with his tongue and hands until she threatened to shout the house down. Tossing her up in the rock brace of his arms, he maneuvered them both into their candlelit bedroom, where he placed her in the center of their canopied bed.

The sheets were thick cotton, scented like roses. The bed was firm, inviting, and loaded with promise. Over the many years of their union they lived dreams, planned goals, cried tears, and made children in that bed, the symbol of their marriage.

And so it was that on this late August night, Sam and Bailey shared their bed once again, only to turn yet another cornerstone in their lives, one made of hope, love, and faith. In the moonlit setting of their bedroom, the possibilities of their union were endless.

Sunday

God Writes Straight
with Crooked Lines

Sixteen

Ridge leaned against the wall of the interrogation room at the New Hope Township police station, his face a blank mask, his dark eyes penetrating. He wore navy slacks, a collarless button down burgundy shirt, a navy leather belt, leather shoes, and socks with burgundy diamonds. It was 10:00 A.M., thirty-six hours since Earl's death.

Tipped by the Walkers and by a secret caller the night before, Ridge had worked with Trinity City police officials, picking up Snake at his one bedroom apartment for questioning about the murder of Earl Stackhouse. The multijurisdiction of police officials between New Hope and Trinity City was running smoothly.

Ridge studied Snake, being careful to note the skinhead's nervous stance, which pleased Ridge. It showed the suspect to be ill-at-ease in the sterile, solemn, frightening confines of the interrogation room. It simplified his task.

The main purpose of the interrogation was to find out Snake's state of mind, his willingness to discuss the murder, his desire to go down alone, or with his comrades. The face-to-face meeting was personal, intense. Body language as well as vocal inflection were critical clues into the suspect's mind. Ridge paid close attention to everything.

The skinhead wore dark blue jeans with straight legs, Nike high tops, and a faded yellow T-shirt. His blonde head was shaved clean except for ragged bangs chopped off just above the eyes. His eyes were green, hard, and full of suspicion.

With a slight upward movement of his right thumb, Ridge signaled for Carlyle to run the small tape recorder on the single table in the chilly room. The Trinity City liaison was on the other side of the two-way mirror, observing the interrogation.

Ridge and Carlyle made sure that all normal police channels were observed so that later prosecution of the suspect would not be hampered by sloppy police work. Ridge wanted Snake and his cronies branded for murder. He worked carefully, slowly, and precisely, as did Carlyle.

The table where Ridge, Carlyle, and Snake sat was a long table of wood, scarred and old. Three hard and uncomfortable ladder-backed chairs sat before the unpolished table. None of the chairs matched the table.

Fluorescent lights cast an eerie glow in the stark, windowless, nearly bare room. Wearing light blue slacks, a light blue short-sleeved Oxford shirt, and tan leather footwear, Carlyle nursed a blue speckled commuter mug filled with caffeinated coffee. His eyes missed nothing.

While Carlyle drank coffee, Ridge chewed a stick of spearmint gum, purely for a devil-may-care effect, as he watched his much sought after, unwilling suspect. The suspect's foot beat a rapid tattoo in the air. The move was a study in male pride, a pride tinged with terror. Ridge was elated with the tattle-tale signs of extreme distress. Things looked good.

Sitting before the two detectives, Snake sweat profusely, all the while reminding himself he was a disciple of Adolf Hitler. Like Hitler, he used brutality to either rid himself of his enemies or at the very least, strike fear into the enemies' heart. Like Hitler, he felt no remorse for the actions he deemed fit or just, although Snake did feel sympathy for himself and his predicament. He kept thinking of Hitler, his hero.

His hero was a gifted man of charisma, a man people followed because they admired the strength of his vision, the surge of his vitality, his ability to dissect and transfix a man, with eyes that could look straight into the dark, naked souls of his believers; people like Satan's Magic, people like Snake.

Scared as he was, sitting between two tough looking cops in a police interrogation room, there was nothing inside Snake that could make him succumb to his own terrible fear of being alone, facing a murder charge.

Like his antihero, Hitler, everything Snake did was calculated, everything he said was filled with self-control, as well as the conviction that his skin color made him right. He focused his mind on his long-gone hero, the only way he could think of to control the urge to squeal on his friends and take the police pressure off himself. He even used his fear as a calculated force.

Inside the sterile interrogation room, an oppressive windowless room where neither sun nor moon ever shone, Snake finally understood Hitler's fascination with the night, understood why Hitler preferred that time of day to draw new believers.

The dark was home to the unconscious mind, to confusion and fear. Snake gathered that fear to him in the way Hitler once gathered followers to him at night. In the dark, a powerful voice could easily be heard; Hitler's voice, Snake's voice.

At night the darkness reinforced Snake's dominance over the rootless people who came to him, believing there was no other place for them to go. In return for his leadership, Snake demanded a raw, gut-level commitment.

Until now, his passion had held Satan's Magic spellbound, as his fiery, racist dogma spilled from every pore of his body, every thought in his mind, every word from his mouth. Like Hitler, Snake was a creator. But Hitler was of no real use to him now; Hitler was dead.

Conjuring up Hitler's speeches, his image, and his vision did not erase Snake's fear. Right now, the windowless interrogation room represented Snake's frightened, trapped, undignified feelings.

Stuck in a jam, he saw what the homicide detectives saw, a racist skinhead on his way to prison. He vowed right then not to go alone. Still, he would not turn Satan's Magic over to the police without a show of pride.

After all, Satan's Magic was his empire, his very own creation. When this empire fell, he would build a new one within the prison system. He would live on, as Hitler lived on through myth and legend. His vision would outlast his fear and his present failure. These final thoughts gave Snake courage.

"What's your real name?" Ridge asked. The silence in the dimly lit room had started screaming; a slow trickle of clear sweat trailed down the suspect's skinny, flushed neck, its pulse beating fast and hard.

Snake's shaved head was tilted to the side, his lips rammed together, his eyes pinched to green slits of disgust. It was a grand performance. "You're the detective, you tell me."

"In time."

Ridge was not sure if Snake's disgust stemmed from his plight, or from being held between two men of color in a house of authority. Ridge liked the odds, which stood on the side of the law.

He knew he and Carlyle made an imposing picture; two large, powerfully built men with heavy silver badges. Ridge's smile showed off the top row of his polished, straight teeth. He felt superb.

Responding to Ridge's calculated, intimidating half-smile, the suspect narrowed his green eyes at the detective, then grinned straight-out, suddenly aware that he and the detective understood each other completely. The suspect relaxed a bit.

Ridge knew Snake would tell him what he and Carlyle wanted to know, but he was not going to make it easy for them. He would make them pull the information from him in slivers in a last attempt at salvaging his deviant pride.

Ridge leaned back in his seat, as if he had all the time in the world. "Ever heard of Earl Stackhouse?" he asked, not expecting a direct answer to his simple question, but asking anyway for the police record.

"No." The word was hard, clipped.

Ridge spoke as casually as if they sat discussing the six o'clock news. "He was murdered Friday night; kicked and bludgeoned to death by a skinhead gang."

Snake stopped fidgeting with his foot. "So?"

Ridge shifted his wad of gum from his left cheek to his right. "I've reason to believe you led the attack."

Snake showed no concern. "Yeah?"

"Yeah."

Snake sneered. "Prove it."

"Before this day is done, I will."

Snake hawked a thin stream of spit into the five-ounce Dixie paper cup which sat to the left of his trembling hand. The gesture was one of pure bravado. Seeing the rude gesture, Ridge visibly calmed himself. Snake was thumbing his nose at Ridge's efforts to hold his temper in check. If the detective lost control, Snake thought, he might be able to use it to his advantage. He spit again.

The detective changed tactics. His tone became intimate, his manner completely sincere, completely at ease. "Do you know that causing another person's death without legal excuse is murder?" he asked, intending to keep Snake off balance with a mixture of easy questions, hard facts, tough accusations, and cajolery.

Snake's eye's flickered with dismay and, for a full second, sheer confusion. "What's a legal excuse?" he asked, wanting to keep the facts of their conversation straight.

Ridge counted off on his strong, hard fingers, calloused

from playing racquetball with Sam. "Self-defense, negli
gent manslaughter, accident." Snake shrugged, though
muscle bunched in his stubbled jaw.

Ridge bit back a smile of victory, aware that his appea
to Snake's ego was beginning to work the way he planned
it to. He had learned early in his career that gang leader
liked recognition of their charisma, a charisma that could
help them lead people into right action as well as wrong
Snake was no exception.

"Are you the leader of Satan's Magic?" he asked, again
quite certain of the answer, once again asking an easy ques
tion for the sake of public record.

Snake flicked his eyes at Carlyle, who sat motionless a
the interrogation table, his intelligent hazel-eyed gaze tak
ing in the crumpled look of Snake's clothes, which looked
clean but slept in. He saw that Snake was not in traditiona
skinhead uniform.

"What if I am the leader?" Snake asked, his tone bel
ligerent, his eyes glassy, his hands clenched so hard tha
his knuckles cracked in the quiet room.

Ridge's devil-may-care look was swept away by a look o
distaste. "I keep track of skinhead gang activities. I dic
some checking around, your gang is new." The velvet
gloved accusation was not lost on the suspect.

A smirk crossed Snake's pale, sweaty face. "Crips and
Bloods run gangs, skins don't. I don't."

Ridge harnessed his energy, sure his patient shift in strat
egy was working on Snake's ego. He had his attention
even though Snake tried to act nonchalant, sure of him
self. Ridge broke down his theory on gangster ethics. Thi
subtle cajolery was a type of coaxing that drew Snake's
reluctant interest. Snake wanted to know what the detec
tive had learned about him and his friends.

"I define a gang as a group of people who commi
crimes based on skin color, culture, sexual value, religion
or territorial rights. Blacks don't run a monopoly on gangs

n Northern California alone there are organized gangs
n the Asian, Hispanic, and Vietnamese communities."

Snake's brows rolled up to a cocky slant. "So?"

Ridge popped his gum. He did it once. He did it twice.
'Until Earl Stackhouse's murder, skinhead activity in this
area was practically nonexistent, even though white supremacist groups exist in Northern California."

Snake assessed Ridge with cold, wary eyes. "You *keep track*
of skins, huh? Funny."

To back his statement, Ridge further proved his expertise to Snake who listened. Intently. "Like most gangs I've
researched, skins use a common name or sign to show
solidarity. Your gang is united by the name Satan's Magic.
You also wear full skin gear in all weather. For instance,
in a heat wave Satan's Magic will wear thick boots and jeans
instead of shorts and sandals."

Snake chuckled, though his amusement did not reach
his frigid green eyes. He studied the short curls on Ridge's
head as if he were meditating on them. *"All weather, huh?"*

Ridge savored Snake's complete, rapt, and cynical attention. He had him jammed up against the wall. "Yes; despite
the unusual heat, all but one of the skins who beat Earl
Stackhouse to death was dressed in full skinhead gear; T-
shirts, jeans, heavy boots, distinctive hair, and tattoos. The
weapons of choice, steel-toed boots and baseball bats, were
typical skinhead arms."

Snake stiffened, as a deer might stiffen at the side of
the road, knowing that danger was close, too close. "What
else do you think you know about skins?" The subtle cajolery had worked.

For all his tough stance, for all his arctic glares, Ridge
decided Snake was strictly amateur. Amateurs often revealed details about themselves and their crimes more easily
than a top criminal with a standard method of operation.
With amateurs, he discovered, there were no hard, swift
rules of conduct.

"Is it true you picked Earl because he was black?" Snak
grunted in response, his eyes shifting everywhere but a
the detective.

Ridge glanced at Carlyle, who telepathed the words, *po*
dirt. "You knew him?"

"Of him," Snake corrected, deciding to come clean, t
perhaps work some beneficial deal with the police, a dea
he might later use in his own defense. He was cornere
and knew it. "There's a difference."

"Explain."

A cunning gleam brightened Snake's green eyes. "What'
in it for me?"

Ridge settled his back against the rungs of his solid woo
seat, his arms folded across his chest. He looked com
posed. "Depends on what you explain."

Snake was silent a minute. "How did you get my name
my address?" They had said nothing about the baseba
bat, but he knew they had it along with his fingerprints
knew they were playing a legal game with him becaus
they wanted to know why Earl had been chosen.

"Anonymous telephone tip last night."

Snake studied first Carlyle, then Ridge. After the pause
he directed his question to Ridge. "Male or female?"

"What do you think?" Ridge countered. He snapped hi
chewing gum.

Carlyle laughed at the worried expression on the sus
pect's face. He laughed because the tough guy was on hi
way down with little more than a token fuss.

Impatient with the detectives, afraid for himself, Snake
grimaced. "If I knew who snitched I wouldn't ask." Hi
expression froze at the sound of someone rapping firmly
on the closed door of the interrogation room.

Carlyle pushed his chair back, its legs scraping loudl
against the linoleum floor. He stood up, crossed the room
opened the door, and inquired. A tall, leggy Eurasia

woman in a crisp blue police uniform stood in the hallway, curiosity on her face.

The woman handed Carlyle what she was carrying in one mauve-tipped hand; a small sheaf of perforated papers, sized 8 1/2 inches wide by 11 inches long. The sheet on top of the short stack of paper was torn at the top right corner, as if it had been ripped when she had torn it off the computer printer.

Carlyle rewarded the attractive woman with a smile, thanked her, then shut the pea-green painted wood door after she had left. He skimmed the papers before nodding his head. "Your f-f-full name is Charles LaVerne Montague?" he asked Snake, his tone amused.

Ridge grinned. "LaVerne?" Snake turned red, but said nothing.

Carlyle continued. "You've got a series of small crimes dating b-b-back to age thirteen. Your arrests relate mostly to larceny; purse snatching, pickpocketing, and items swiped from c-c-cars."

"Busy boy," Ridge noted out loud. "Why murder, Snake?"

The suspect groaned, all attempts at bravado dashed to pieces. "We didn't mean for him to die." At this point of the interrogation, Snake only cared about saving his own hide. In truth, he felt no remorse for his crime.

Ridge pressed. "You admit it?"

Snake stared at the water stained ceiling. For the hundredth time he wished he had thought to wear surgical gloves to the boot party. He knew as well as the police did that his fingerprints were the only ones on the recovered murder weapon. The legal game was over.

"Why not?" Snake asked, sarcasm lending a sharp edge to his voice, a sarcasm that was all show, all bravado, considering he felt scared enough to release his bowels. "You've got my fingerprints because I dropped my baseball bat last night. I assume you've got it stashed away around here somewhere?"

"Under lock and key. Besides the baseball bat, some body squealed on you, Snake, somebody you know," Ridge said, reminding Snake of the anonymous tip, reminding him that he was in trouble, and all by himself, unless he came clean with useful information.

Snake drummed his fingers against the worn tabletop, its wood gouged with obscene words. "Male or female?" he asked again.

"What's your best guess?" Ridge prodded.

Snake's lip pursed together as if he were tasting something nasty, something tart, something he never wanted to taste again. He thought of Digits, Holiday, Bash, Grip, Tommy Gun, and Head Hunter. "I've got two people in mind."

Ridge stopped snapping his gum. "Give me names."

"I need to think." His complaint was flustered.

"You've got ten minutes. In ten minutes, I'm booking you for the murder of Earl Stackhouse."

Snake breathed in deeply, his chest heaving with the effort. "What degree?"

"That isn't up to me."

"Guess."

"Either first or second degree, possibly second."

Snake shifted in his seat. He put both palms on the table and both feet on the floor. His knees were spread wide, his shoulders stiff, square. The bare room was ripe with his fear. "What's the difference?" he asked.

Ridge pushed the skin back on the cuticles of his left hand with the sturdy thumbnail of his right hand. "Murder in the first degree is when someone kills with deliberation. It's punished by life imprisonment or death."

"And?"

"Murder in the second degree is when someone kills a

a result of an intent to harm but not murder. Punishment for murder in the second is no picnic."

Snake let the detective's reply sink in before asking, "How did you find me if you didn't know my true name until a few moments ago?"

Ridge blew another bubble. When it popped, he blew another. "Surveillance."

Snake's eyes widened when he realized just how long he had been spied on by the police. He looked alert, nervous as a gopher on the run in someone's backyard. He looked trapped. He had not worried when Head Hunter and Tommy Gun told him about the couple in the minivan. He saw now he should have worried about a lot of little things.

"Your kidding?" he asked, though the detectives knew that Snake already knew the answer by the quiet, bewildered way he asked his question.

Ridge almost laughed at the shocked look on Snake's face. "Not hardly, we've tracked you ever since you left Club X last night."

Snake's mind reeled as he relived the night before. He had left Club X with Tommy Gun, Head Hunter, Grip, Bash, Holiday, and Digits. They had gone to his apartment for an orgy of sex and wild conversation about the coming race war.

Before dawn, Snake had kicked everybody out, as was his custom. He never liked waking up to hangovers or embarrassed faces, never liked waking up to realize that race wars went on every day, and that he was not so original after all.

"Phone taps?" he asked, after clearing his throat. Due to his incredible, escalating fear, he no longer had enough spit to toss inside the Dixie cup.

"No."

Snake considered every movie he'd ever seen on television about police surveillance. "Then you've got pictures of the people I was with?" Head Hunter said the couple took a picture of Club X, but maybe it was more than that. Maybe they were detectives.

Ridge's response was cryptic. "What do you think?" Snake glanced at Carlyle, who winked.

"I think I'm in deep."

Ridge nearly smiled at his victory. "Very deep."

At this point, Snake was clearly agitated. A nerve beneath his left eye twitched, his fingers drummed against the long, scarred table. Sweat fell from the pits of his arms, forming rings on his faded yellow T-shirt. "I need to think."

Ridge obliged him. "Your ten minutes haven't started yet. When they do, remember this; there is motive, opportunity, and evidence that connects you to the Stackhouse murder. You can go down alone or not alone. The choice is yours, Charles LaVerne Montague, but you will go down."

Ridge glanced at his watch. "You've got ten minutes, starting now." Thus said, he silently reviewed the facts of the murder as he leaned back in his seat to study the hair on the rough side of his knuckles.

The motive for the crime was race. The opportunity to commit the crime came in a nearly deserted strip mall parking lot. The evidence linking the crime with one of the suspects was a baseball bat with incriminating fingerprints, Snake's fingerprints.

Ridge also had eyewitnesses, who all agreed to testify against the skinheads, and who all believed they would recognize the skinheads in a police line up. He could hardly wait to tell the Walkers.

Meanwhile, the skinheads in Snake's apartment were freaking out.

"Snake was arrested!" Holiday declared, stunned. She wore her blonde hair in a ponytail at the base of her skull. She wore a T-shirt, jeans, and military boots. The air was hot around her, stifling and cloying, like the fear in her eyes.

She and the rest of Satan's Magic were in Snake's small apartment. Closed up, the apartment retained the three scents peculiar to their Saturday night group gatherings: stale beer, stale sweat, and stale sex.

Wearing military boots, light blue jeans, and a ribbed tank top, Bash sneered at Holiday, his mind unwilling to trust the worried look on her face. "Snake said he's in jail 'cause one of you bitches probably snitched on him. He called from the jail house to warn us."

Looking stiff and wary in scuffed running shoes, navy jeans, and a ripped T-shirt, Grip shook his head. "Maybe he called to set us up."

Digits frowned. She was dressed identically to Holiday, only she wore her brunette hair loose about her shoulders. "What?"

"Snake called Bash from the jail house. Bash called us. We all met here. Maybe we shouldn't be here," Grip said, knowing full well he was the man who tipped the police anonymously the night before from the pay phone at Club X.

Bash was uneasy, but loyal. "No, Snake wanted us together so we can figure out what to do next. He ain't about to turn us in to no cops."

Grip stared at Bash in disbelief. "Snake is in jail, about to be charged with murder. He'll talk."

Uncertain about what to do, Bash slammed one crushing fist against one sweaty palm. "I wish I knew who snitched. It had to be one of us, but who?"

"It could've been Tommy Gun or Head Hunter," Holiday suggested, her brow furrowed, distressed to think someone in Satan's Magic may have confessed during the orgy held once they had left Club X. The latest recruits were not present for this latest revelation in the drama that was their lives because they had not been in the boot party. This meeting was private.

Digits supported her oldest friend now, as she did in most cases. "She's right. Why would one of us get Snake arrested when there's so much to lose? For all we know, it could have been you who turned Snake in to the cops. You don't keep it a secret you want to run joint command of Satan's Magic during the race wars." Bash glared at her.

"Maybe you even got tired of waiting around for Snake to act," Holiday said, backing Digits up. "Maybe you even wanted to get rid of Snake so you can take first command. Maybe you even thought that, with Snake taking the fall for murder, the heat would be off of us. Maybe Snake is dead and you're lying to us now. We only have your word that he's in jail."

Digits said, "She's telling the truth."

Bash raised his hand to smack Digits for being right, but Grip stopped him in mid-arc, saying, "It was a matter of time before the police caught on to Snake and you know it, Bash. It's his bat that was left behind at the minimart. His fingerprints are all over it."

"I'm getting outta here," Holiday declared. Nobody tried to stop her when she dived for her purse.

Digits refused to hang around either. "Me, too."

Bash did not know what to do. He wanted to run, only he had no place to go. "Hold it, you two. We're in this thing together."

Grip stated calmly, "Not anymore. Somebody broke into your apartment yesterday. I don't like it. Me and the girls are leaving. You do what you want." He motioned for Holiday and Digits to join him at the front door.

Bash looked at Grip, wondering why he was so calm. Suddenly it hit him why the other man took the news of Snake's arrest so easily. "You!" Bash hollered, as soon as Grip's fingertips had touched the front doorknob.

Grip froze. Bash knew he was right about his gut feeling. He pointed an accusing finger. "You're the one who snitched!"

Loud banging on Snake's apartment door halted Bash's slow, menacing advance on Grip, who was simply standing there, waiting for the confrontation. Holiday raced to the keyhole.

"Police!" she hissed, pure fear in her eyes. "What do we do?"

Digits never waited for an answer. She left. Moving quickly, she ran to the bathroom. Jumping on top of the dirty commode, she shoved the narrow window above it open to its widest position.

Breathing hard, she hauled herself up and over the ledge just as the police rammed open Snake's front door. She hit the dirt below so hard her jaw rattled at the joints. With a quick roll to her feet, she took off for her car in a dead run.

In Snake's apartment, Grip prayed she had got away as, with both hands up, he surrendered to the Trinity City Police, arrest and search warrants in full view. Bash resisted arrest. Holiday screamed. The police searched for Digits.

Tires squealing from the alley confirmed to Ridge and Carlyle that one of the women had escaped, as reported by the arresting police team via walkie-talkie. A Trinity City patrol car was speeding after the old Thunderbird as soon as it hit the first corner. Ridge and Carlyle followed in close pursuit.

"Hot d-d-damn!" Carlyle hollered as he yanked loose his paisley silk tie.

Digits drove erratically, desperate, knowing that twin police cars pushed hot on her tail. She hit curbs, ran stop lights, careened around corners as she headed for the closest freeway. She gunned the car south toward the one safe place she could think of: home. Ridge and Carlyle were right behind her.

Carlyle processed the suspect's license plate through standard police procedure, via radio, to confirm what he and Ridge already knew. A vital confirmation of the vehicle was his way of sticking to protocol regarding probable cause to arrest.

Ridge listened to the radio confirmation of the license plate and muttered, "Lord, have mercy, Sam was right. He cracked the case."

"Hot d-d-damn!" Carlyle hollered again, as upset as Ridge about their expected destination. "This is the k-k-kind of stuff that makes me want to quit the force."

"You and me both," Ridge muttered as he watched the speeding Thunderbird. "You and me both."

In the Thunderbird, Digits scarcely breathed as she exited the freeway. She accelerated harder two blocks from home. She made it. Slamming the gear into park, she flung open the driver side door, Carlyle and Ridge right behind her, their siren blaring.

Parked at the nearest corner to the Stackhouse home were Sam and Bailey in the family van. They had been watching the yellow house in case the Thunderbird returned. When they saw the old car barrelling down the street, its driver screeching to a halt in front of the Stackhouse home, they both jumped from their van to pursue on foot.

Nearly blind with tears at the inevitable, Digits ran to the open front door of her house, and straight into her stepfather's arms. Instinctively, protectively, he grabbed her to his chest. Abruptly, he let her go.

"Wendy!" Donna Stackhouse screamed, alarmed by the sounds of police sirens, alarmed by the Walkers racing fast across her lawn, two police officers close on their heels.

"Wendy Goddard," Ridge announced, his badge glinting in the sun, "you're under arrest for suspicion of murder." Wendy was Digits, Earl's half-sister.

Wendy's sapphire-colored gaze burned into the matching gaze of her stricken mother. "Mama, I'm sorry. I didn't mean . . . didn't want . . . I'm sorry, Mama."

"Don't you dare say you're sorry to me!" Donna screamed.

Wendy touched her mother's arm. Donna pulled away, slapping her soundly, the single, damning act expressing the sheer bitterness of her sorrow. In tears, Donna sank to the floor, repelled by her own flesh and blood.

Anguish, then disgust fled across Melvin's face as he stared at Wendy. Flinging her selfish, grasping fingers away from him, he picked up his wife from the foyer where she lay crumpled in despair. Clasping her trembling body against his chest, he carried her away, determined to salvage their shattered love.

Epilogue

A Hair in the Butter

It was two weeks later, a Sunday in New Hope. Bailey pulled her red cotton apron off and then carried a pound cake to the table on the veranda. To make the pound cake she had sifted together flour, baking soda, baking powder, and salt in a medium-sized mixing bowl.

In a larger bowl, she creamed butter, sugar, and vanilla. Into this mixture she had added eggs. She had poured the dry ingredients into the creamed mixture and stirred with an electric beater. She had put the batter in a greased, fluted cake pan to bake until the top was golden brown. The finished cake smelled wonderful. It was a favorite of Sam's.

Dressed in light gray shorts and a geometric print shirt, Sam settled the small skirmish between Fern and Sage over which video game they would play first on their Sega in the den. When he finished, he joined Bailey and Ridge on the covered veranda, where they were nibbling dessert and drinking tea. It was raining.

"Have you guys noticed the similarity between this adventure and the one we had the first time we met?" Bailey asked the men, her body comfortable in faded jean shorts and a floral print top.

"Come to think of it, yeah," Sam agreed, recalling how Ridge responded to an attack on Bailey during her investigation of the death of her friend, Mary Lou Booker.

Dressed in khaki walking shorts and matching polo shirt, Ridge pointed out the similarities. "In both cases, there was a mysterious death and a closed circle of suspects."

Bailey toyed with her glass. "One major difference be-

tween this murder mystery and the last one is that Sam
was driven to solve the case instead of me. Both cases began with a feast, only in this case there were skeletons at
the feast instead of friends."

Ridge frowned. "What?"

"You know. On the surface, New Hope is a beautiful
town full of beautiful people, but every now and then
something happens to remind us that the beauty we see
is only an ideal. I mean, New Hope is a feast of opportunity
for people of color. This town is low on crime, high on
achievement, rich in culture."

"Almost a fantasy," Sam concurred.

"Exactly. The skinheads showed me that no matter how
beautiful this town and its people are, we still have ugly
secrets."

Sam nodded. "Skeletons."

"Exactly, and in this case there were skeletons at the
feast of life."

Enjoying the cool, wet afternoon, in the company of two
handsome men, with the familiarity of her children arguing in the background, Bailey looked at Sam, her mind at
peace. "This conversation is so Agatha Christie."

He laughed. "How?"

"Well, I was thinking about her book, *The Murder of Roger
Ackroyd*. The book ends with an explanation of the reasons
behind the murders committed inside the story."

Ridge's eyes lit up. "She did the same thing in *Appoint-
ment with Death*."

"Aah," Sam murmured, "a trademark."

Bailey smiled. "Yes, it helps clear up the loose ends that
developed in her murder mysteries, the way we're doing
now."

Ridge turned serious. "It shocked me to discover that
one of the women I interviewed, Elsie Goddard, was first
cousin to Earl's mother, Donna Goddard Stackhouse. The

two women in the skinhead gang, Holiday and Digits, were cousins.

"Digits, whose real name is Wendy Goddard, was Earl's older half-sister. They shared the same mother, but different fathers. Holiday, whose real name is Rachel, is Elsie Goddard's daughter.

"It appears that nobody in the Goddard family got along too well. Elsie and Rachel Goddard were outcasts in their family because of the men they played around with sometimes. Elsie has a penchant for men of color that conflicts with her supremacist upbringing, an upbringing which made taboo men even more appealing.

"Elsie's conflicts affected her daughter, Holiday, turning her into a fence straddler between the racist and nonracist worlds. Holiday is not of mixed heritage. The fence straddling, outsider persona forged a bond between Holiday and her cousin, Digits."

Fingering the dip bowl on the table, Sam said, "It's amazing the way genetics work. Who'd ever guess Earl and Wendy were related?"

His elbows on the table, Ridge explained. "When Melvin met Donna, she was a single mother. Digits's father didn't claim her, nor did he ever marry her mother. After a time, against both their families' wishes, Melvin married Donna. Together they had Earl, a dark-skinned child with blue eyes. Digits was jealous."

"Why?" Bailey asked, appalled by the broken family ties in Earl's home.

Ridge took a sip from his frosted glass of sweet iced tea. 'It's complex. Digits never forgave her father for not claiming her, which was why she resented Earl's relationship with Melvin, a man who claimed his child.

"She also never forgave her mother for embarrassing her by making a black man her stepfather, the reason she felt like a misfit in normal society. Feeling like a misfit sent her into Satan's Magic. Remember, the Goddard family is rooted in white supremacy."

Sam grimaced over the twisted mess. "What I don't understand is how Wendy's parents didn't know she was in a gang."

Ridge explained. "She kept a duffel bag of gang clothes in the trunk of her car. She had no tattoos or anything else permanent that would peg her as a gang member."

Bailey shook her head in dismay. "She was terribly insecure."

Ridge agreed. "She placed her insecure feelings about her real family into a pseudo family of skinheads, a group of people who were as unforgiving as she was unforgiving of things she could never change. Digits felt more powerful in the pseudo family than she did in her real family."

Sam swept a few lilac blossoms from the arm of his chair. "Earl could never change the way he looked. He could never be common, the very thing Wendy must have despised most about herself. She was not overtly remarkable."

Bailey swept her eyes over the herbs in her garden, their scent released into the air by the late summer rain. "When I heard Wendy telling her mother she was sorry, I wanted to slap her myself. What nerve."

Ridge broke his lemon rind into pieces, knowing it would find its way into the compost pile Bailey kept to fertilize her garden. "God writes straight with crooked lines. We don't always know why people fight things they don't have power to change, like Wendy not making peace with her heritage."

Sam took a sip of iced tea before saying, "Yeah, God writes straight, meaning He's fair. The lines are crooked because His reasons aren't always understood. Even though justice was served to the skinheads, the victory is not a straight one because there are no real winners. The bad guys aren't so much cold-blooded killers as they are misfits in society."

Bailey cast her gaze over the distant hillside, her expression troubled. "But why did she have Earl beaten to death?"

Ridge answered. "First of all, they were high on drugs and alcohol. Second, Earl's death was not planned. Digits and Earl had an argument the day he died. Apparently, he'd told their parents she'd been sneaking out at night.

"What he hadn't told them, but was thinking about telling them, was that she was sneaking out to be with adult men, Snake, Grip, and Bash, who Digits and Holiday met at Club X. Both Digits and her cousin are minors."

Sam got the gist of things. "So Wendy wanted to threaten Earl into silence. If he told his parents she was sleeping with men, the men she slept with would go to jail. Wendy's relationship with the skinhead gang was as complex and disturbing as her relationship with her real family."

"True," Ridge agreed. "Digits approached Snake about the boot party to silence Earl. The rest you know," he added.

Bailey's heart felt heavy. "Did Snake have any idea Earl and Wendy were related?"

"No."

"But wouldn't Snake question why the girls wanted to jump him?"

Ridge took another sip of cold, sweet tea before answering her question. "Digits and Holiday told Snake that Earl was uppity for a black boy. Snake needed no other reason."

Sam leaned back in his seat, his legs sprawled. "Why do you think Elsie Goddard cooperated with us, if she knew her daughter was an accomplice to murder?"

"Elsie Goddard and Rachel, aka Holiday, weren't close, probably because the adult-child relationship wasn't clear. Elsie went to Club X, knowing her minor daughter also went to Club X. Holiday didn't respect her mother, but she did respect and trust Digits, her best friend and cousin. Elsie's bond with Donna ran along the same, but weaker, lines. In a warped, indirect way, she was helping Donna."

"I don't get it," Sam admitted, thinking about the Goddard family mess. "Elsie and Donna are first cousins. They were family."

Ridge explained. "Neither Donna's family nor Melvin'
family liked the idea of Donna and Melvin's marriage
Donna lives in a mostly black neighborhood because sh
says that community is more accepting of her relationshi
with Melvin, and generally more accepting of her children

"Wendy didn't like that either, another reason she re
belled against her parents by joining a racist gang. Digit
carried on the tradition of intolerance she inherited from
the Goddard family. Nothing about that family is simple."

Bailey poured a fresh round of iced tea. "So just thre
blocks away, a young brother and sister battled each othe
until one of them died. They were siblings by nature's law
not by emotion, which was why Wendy was disconnecte
enough from Earl to plan the boot party that ultimatel
killed him."

Bailey drew a deep breath, then expelled it slowly. "
guess it was tough for Wendy to grow up in a biracial famil
Two children: one black, one white; two parents: one black
one white. No wonder Donna and Melvin didn't have mor
kids."

"I agree," Ridge replied. "If they produced anothe
child like Earl, Digits would flip."

Having learned more about the Stackhouses in the pa
week, Sam thought he understood the source of Earl
peace during the conflict that killed him. "So Earl hid i
his books while Wendy hid in trouble?"

"You got it," Ridge answered, running a finger along th
arm of his wrought iron seat. "Earl's outlet brought hi
comfort and peace. Digits's outlet brought her pain an
grief."

"What's gonna happen to Wendy?" Sam asked.

"That's up to a judge and jury."

Sad, Bailey hugged herself. "I feel so sorry for Earl
parents."

Ridge focused on Bailey. "At their daughter's arraig
ment, I watched those two. There's a lot of love an

strength between them. They've held tough against the bigots in their family and in society. I believe they'll make it through the coming trial."

Sam lowered his lids to mask the fiery expression in his black eyes. "I feel as if my entire belief system has been challenged."

Bailey tried to interpret Sam's closed look, his tight demeanor, his cryptic words. "What do you mean?"

His anger was a palpable thing. "It's hard to be positive when the skinheads who killed Earl are gonna get a fair trial through the court system, even after they confessed to his murder and were positively identified as his killers. I don't want them to have any rights."

Ridge met his friend's turbulent gaze. "In a free society, Sam, everyone has rights, even killers. The price for that freedom means we deal with the good and bad actions and opinions of every person in this country. Whether we like it or not, extremists have the right to do or say what they please."

Sam's fist clenched around his glass. The ice tumbled inside, making a clinking sound. "Extremists are a self-serving minority group. They should be ostracized."

Ridge studied Sam's profile. "We need the courts."

"Too slow," Sam argued. "The newspaper says that Satan's Magic's leader, Snake, used racist speeches to brainwash them into following him. Is that true?"

Ridge said, "It's true. Snake did push them with racist speeches. He used them as a sort of backstairs influence. By that I mean a subtle control over his peers. It was through his peers, his gang, that he was strong."

Sam was clearly skeptical. "I don't think his followers should be able to say he used violent words to brainwash them into killing Earl."

Ridge drew upon his background in criminal law. "We're talking thin lines and complicated interpretations of the law. If we ban unpopular speech because we don't like it, then we violate somebody's right to say what he thinks."

Her brows drawn into lines of concentration, Bailey argued the point. "But you agree that it was wrong for Snake to use racist speeches to incite his followers."

"I say it's wrong because the U.S. Supreme Court says it's wrong," Ridge explained. "According to the law, fighting words are as bad as obscenity or libel or treason. What's hard to do is to decide what exactly are fighting words. That's one reason why the skinheads need to go through the judicial system."

Bailey shook her head. "I don't think there will ever be an end to racism. It's taught to children in every generation. Look at what happened to Wendy and Rachel Goddard."

"Every generation also teaches tolerance," Ridge added. "It sometimes takes a tragedy like Earl's death to spark the most meaningful responses within a community."

Sam's face was solemn. "That much is true. It happened here when Quentin flew the flag at half mast, and again when he called a neighborhood meeting."

"Don't downplay your role as amateur detectives. I don't like the idea of private citizens taking the law into their own hands, but not only did you guys track down the skinheads, you did a great job leading the community meeting."

Bailey grinned. "I'd say we led a separate but parallel investigation to yours, the common goal being the capture of the skinheads. Now, with the rain, I feel we're headed toward happier days. It's time for the rainbow. I'm ready."

Ridge lifted his glass in a toast. "Speaking of fresh starts, I've resigned from the police force."

Concerned by the guarded expression on his face, Bailey placed a hand on his forearm. "Why? You love your job."

"Answering that question is like picking a strand of hair off the top of warm butter. Just say, I've been thinking about a career change for more than a year. The change isn't sudden."

"But how will you earn a living?" she quizzed.

"I'll turn my hobby of refinishing old furniture into a full time business. I've got plenty of money invested and saved, so a year without a regular paycheck won't hurt. Earl's death is the latest in a string of reminders of how much I need to live a good life. No more being a workaholic."

Bailey turned her worried gaze on her friend. "This all sounds so strange."

"It is and it isn't," he explained. "I've got a house I only sleep in, plus a relaxing hobby that could turn a profit if I only had the time to pursue it. Quitting the police force will give me that time. I'm ready."

Disgruntled, Sam posed a question of his own. "It's gotta be the family thing."

Ridge paused, alert to the intense throb in Sam's voice. "What family thing?"

"Me and Bailey and the kids. You feel left out, don't you?"

"Good grief, Sam!" Bailey exclaimed, aware the atmosphere between the men was suddenly charged. "Ridge is—"

"A lonely man," Ridge finished. For him, the truth had a sting to it.

Sam studied him with cool black eyes. Earl's death had brought to light yet another secret: the unspoken, shared love of Bailey. Like the simmering racism the gang beating unsurfaced, their love for the same woman was now in the open. They had to deal with it.

"Maybe it is time you got your own woman and settled down."

"Sam!" Bailey squealed as she lightly punched his arm. Even so, the methodical wheels of the born matchmaker spun in her pretty little head.

Ignoring her shocked gasp, Ridge met Sam's look. Neither man glanced at Bailey who sat between them with her mouth hanging open. "I want a woman who'll be as good to me as she is to you."

Hot jealousy burst in Sam's chest now that the unspoken was spoken at last. In the next instant, he realized he and Ridge were too much alike not to want the same kind of woman; strong, beautiful, and gifted. The big men eyed each other across the patio table, sizing each other up.

Bailey watched the men watch each other and wondered how anybody as nosy as she was could be so blind. She never once thought about Ridge in a romantic way, but as she studied the broad shouldered men on either side of her, she never felt so adored.

These men were proud warriors, men willing to use their natural power to defend, to protect, and to cherish the women and children who trusted them without condition, the way she, Fern, and Sage trusted them.

Bailey marveled that both men were hers for keeps; one in friendship, the other in love. With one palm on each man's bicep, she grinned broadly at them both before tossing a calculating glance at Ridge. The look worried him.

Ready for some serious matchmaking, she had the perfect candidate in mind for him; the very original, equally lovely Miss Vancy McKay. Bailey beamed at her guest. "How about attending a little dinner party after you settle in to your new career?"

Alarmed, Sam's eyes collided with Ridge's over the top of her rose scented hair. "Oh no!" the men said together. They were now two men banded together against a matchmaking woman.

Bailey laughed, delighted they were not too sure about what to do about her good intentions. "Don't worry fellas," she assured them, giving each man a squeeze on the arm, "I've got it all under control."

Groaning loudly in protest, they just bet she did.

Bailey's Recipes

Spaghetti

2 pounds mild Italian sausage, the casing removed, the
  sausage rolled into small balls
1 pound ground beef
1 onion
3 cloves of garlic
2 tablespoons dried parsley
2 tablespoons dried basil
2 tablespoons dried oregano
1 teaspoon salt
3/4 teaspoon pepper
3 teaspoons sugar
1 12-ounce can of tomato paste
1 28-ounce can of crushed tomatoes
1 1/4 cups water
1 cup burgundy wine
vegetable oil

1 small package of spaghetti
1 cup parmesan cheese, shredded
2 tablespoons of butter
1 teaspoon parsley

Brown beef in a medium skillet. Brown sausage in vegetable oil in a large skillet with a lid. While the meat is cooking, chop the vegetables up fine (Bailey uses a Black &
Decker Handy Chopper). Drain the meat. Put the meat
and vegetables in a large pot. Add the rest of the ingredients. Stir. Heat on medium until sauce bubbles, then sim-
mer very low for two hours, stirring occasionally.

Prepare spaghetti noodles according to package. Drain
noodles. Rinse them quickly with cool water. Return to
pot. Stir in butter, parsley, and parmesan cheese. Serve
noodles hot with meat sauce on top.

*Bailey seasons the spaghetti noodles because Fern likes them without sauce.

French Bread

6 1/2 cups flour
2 1/2 cups warm water
1 teaspoon vegetable oil
2 packages of yeast
1 teaspoon sugar
1 tablespoon salt
1 tablespoon cold water
1 egg white
yellow cornmeal
vegetable shortening

Put the yeast, salt, sugar, and two cups of flour in a large mixing bowl. Add the oil and warm water. Beat well with electric mixer. Add the rest of the flour in two cup increments, stirring with a spoon. Put dough on a floured board. Knead dough for fifteen minutes, adding up to a half cup of flour if needed to make a stiff dough. Place dough in a greased bowl. Flip dough over so that the greased bottom is now on top inside the bowl. Cover bowl with a clean dish towel. Let it rise until doubled (about an hour).

Divide dough into two balls. Shape the balls into the traditional French bread look (a rectangle with round ends). Put the dough on cookie sheets that are smeared with vegetable shortening and sprinkled with yellow cornmeal. Cut three diagonal slits across the top of the bread, 1/8" deep, roughly 3" apart. Cover with dish towel. Let rise until doubled (about an hour).

In a small bowl, combine egg white and cold water. Baste this mixture over the unbaked loaves of bread. Bake loaves at 375 degrees until golden brown.

*Bailey lets the bread cool enough to handle without a mitt, slices it through the center with a bread knife, coats the inside of the bread with plain butter or with garlic butter spread, puts the halves back together, slices the bread into single serving pieces, then wraps the bread in foil. The warm bread is served with dinner.

Author's Acknowledgements

Carolyn Willis, hairstylist extraordinaire, of Carolyn's Hair Salon in Antioch, California. Carolyn worked miracles on my self-permed, self-cut head. She also single-handedly promoted Arabesque books in a city where these wonders are scarce. Monique Gilmore for sharing her writer's savvy and wonderful friendship; Antoinette Reed for the fabulous Girls Only weekend in May; Joanne Buckley for reviving in me the joys of tea between women friends on quiet mornings alone without kids; Tamara Lewis, for opening her home to family and friends for a private, meaningful guest appearance at her women's reading club, Nia-Imani; Karen Harrington, for countless trips to the bookstores on behalf of her many friends, and for putting a hold on the munchies while she stayed with me at Barnes and Noble; Toni and Kim for reading those early rough drafts (I do mean rough); Steve, for literally standing at my side without complaining for hours at a time during my brief, intense booksigning tour; Steven, for telling anybody who will listen when my books hit the shelves; Randal, for all those great ideas you have to get me going when my thinking slows down. To everyone who wrote letters to me about *Delicious,* thank you. Not only did I learn from them, I treasure them all.

Dear Readers,

Attending a wedding last year, I noticed a young man with light brown skin, light brown hair, and dark blue eyes. I'd never seen blue eyes on a black person until then. I'm very aware that black people have eyes in shades of blue, gray, and green. It's the idea of seeing a stunning and clear shade of blue, gray, or green when least expected that inspired this story.

Please let me know what you thought about *Sensation*. To finish off the Sam and Bailey Walker Trilogy, I'm writing a story about Ridge Williams. He finally meets the woman of his dreams, Vancy McKay. I hope you'll like her, too.

If you'll send your letter with a business size, self-addressed stamped envelope, I'll be sure to write you back. Please mail your response to *Sensation* by way of my publisher, who will forward your letters to me. Here's the address:

Shelby Lewis
C/O Monica Harris
Kensington Publishing Corporation
850 Third Avenue
New York, NY 10022

Sincerely yours,
Shelby Lewis

Turn the page for an exciting excerpt from

BEWITCHING,

Part Three in the Walker Trilogy

One

Vancy McKay never spent much time thinking about marriage. "Bailey you need to quit, girl," she told her good friend since grade school.

Enjoying her conversation with Vancy, Bailey sat at the farm-style table in her multi-windowed nook. She wore a pair of faded blue jeans and her husband's old gray sweatshirt which hung an inch past her behind, still firm after two children and a part-time catering business she ran from home.

"You don't have to marry Ridge, Vancy. You just have to meet him," Bailey advised, her voice so chipper Vancy grimaced. "I told him the same thing."

A health nut with a sweet tooth, Vancy tossed back a handful of carob coated raisins. They were tasty. "Everybody knows blind dates don't work," she garbled, though the tone of her words remained emphatic.

Bailey wiggled her crimson painted toes before the portable heater at her feet. It was mid-September in New Hope, California. That meant it was too hot to start the main heater in the big farmhouse, too cold not to know autumn danced around the proverbial corner. "Girl, you are more than plain stubborn, you're pigheaded."

"And you're not?" Vancy challenged, thinking back to the many scrapes she and Bailey had been grounded for as kids growing up in the same middle-class neighborhood.

The grandest childhood escapade Vancy could remem-

ber was the time she and Bailey had smuggled jumbo marsh-
mallows into their sleeping bags during an overnight Girl
Scouts' camping trip. They had woken to an army of tiny
ants, but each girl had refused to admit foul play. They had
been grounded a week by their parents for their mischief.

Bailey toyed with the handle of her white coffee mug,
embossed with a green bell pepper split down its middle.
Instead of coffee, she drank hot chocolate with huge marsh-
mallows melting across the steamy, sweet top. "We're not
talking about me. Besides, you're the one saying too many
men are bad news. I just want you to meet one of the good
guys."

Vancy snorted, caring little that it was not an elegant
sound. She was glad her new age retail store stood empty
for a minute or two, the reason she could kick back in her
emerald-colored crushed velvet chair, her size-ten feet
propped on a tapestry-covered footstool.

"There aren't too many men like Sam," she praised her
long time friend. "When you find one like him, call me
up."

"I'm calling you up."

"Girl, please."

Vancy twirled her red painted fingernails around the
dark cord of her French style telephone, its gold embel-
lishments gleaming under the store's soft ceiling lights.
Back in the ninth grade she had been the friend who
turned Bailey on to red nail polish, a habit that had stuck.

"So you'll come?" Bailey asked, her tone more a tease
than a question. She knew full well Vancy was too curious
not to attend her intimate dinner party. She had invited
only treasured friends: Vancy, Minette, Lucinda, Ridge,
Victor, and Charles. As hosts, she and Sam completed the
circle of eight.

Vancy sucked in a deep breath of jasmine scented incense. She burned the relaxing scent all day long in her

metaphysical store. She liked the holistic approach to life.
"Depends on what you're making for dinner."

Bailey told her with a flourish. "Broiled lobster tails,
baked potatoes, cheddar cheese dinner rolls, a squash
medley, and pineapple salad with peach cobbler for dessert. So are you coming now?"

"Wild horses couldn't keep me away," Vancy replied,
sounding as if her life depended on that single meal. Over
the years she had become addicted to Bailey's rich, tasty,
come-back-for-more food.

Bailey chuckled. She knew full well Vancy loved whatever
she served for dinner. It was why she selected those par-
ticular dishes. Vancy was a sucker for lobster tails dipped
in hot butter, potatoes cooled with sour cream, and peach
cobbler made from scratch.

More unorganized than she cared to admit, Vancy tossed
a wad of sales receipts into the teddy bear cookie jar she
kept under the service counter. Only that morning, her
tax accountant had threatened to take her business else-
where if Vancy did not get her act together when it came
to organizing her store's sales, citing that the cookie jar
system was tough to work with.

"Tell me again who else is coming?" Vancy inquired
softly.

Bailey's grin came across in her voice as she reeled her
friend in for dinner. "Minette and Victor. Charles and—"

"Ooh that man is fine," Vancy interrupted, her husky
voice dragging out the ooh.

Bailey stopped swinging her toes long enough to ask
quickly, "Which man? Victor or Charles?"

"Victor is more fine than last night's wine." Built like a
distance runner, he stood just under six feet, and he
adored Minette Ramsey, another reason Vancy liked him
a lot. He pursued Minette relentlessly, a fact Vancy and
Bailey had only recently discovered. Charles and his wife,
Lucinda, were as solid as Bailey and Sam.

Bailey's voice sunk to a conspiratorial tone that was so enticing to Vancy she sat up straighter in her crushed velvet seat, pressed the French phone hard against her amethyst studded ear, and held her breath as Bailey finally dropped her bomb, "Victor asked Minette to marry him."

Vancy screamed. "No, he didn't!"

"Yes, he did!"

"So when is the wedding?" Vancy asked as she settled her five-foot-nine-inch body into the curve of her cushy chair.

As always, Vancy enjoyed gossiping with Bailey. They never tried to hurt anyone with their chatty ways. They simply enjoyed keeping each other informed of the latest skinny among their peers.

"You tell me," Bailey said, loving all the juicy flavor of their early morning chit chat.

"Girl, please. Don't tell me Minette didn't holler yes at the top of her lungs?" Victor was rich, filthy rich.

Bailey slurped a sip of hot chocolate. "Okay, I won't tell you."

Vancy tossed back another handful of carob coated raisins before muttering, "Is she crazy?"

"Nervous," Bailey replied, all matter of fact and filled with concern even though she had burned her tongue with the chocolate.

Cupping the phone between her left shoulder and ear, she stirred the marshmallow into her drink. It was good timing because Vancy was temporarily bereft of words, her mouth at work on her raisins.

As she stirred with a mint handled teaspoon, Bailey recognized that she and Minette were as strong together as she and Vancy, but for different reasons. Minette was solid, sentimental, and protective. Vancy was vivacious, witty, and very unique.

"Nervous about what?" Vancy asked, clearly puzzled.

The frown she wore came across in her husky, trademark voice.

"Failing at marriage a second time around," Bailey reminded her friend.

They both knew all the particulars about Minette's break up, but believed Minette was strong enough to get over the hurdle of her shattered marriage with the man who had beaten her when he felt low.

"Victor Griffin is a long way from Minette's ex-husband, Judd."

Bailey waved her feet in front of the small, handy portable heater she carried with her around the house when she needed it. "Victor is a patient man."

Vancy did not believe that for one second. She had known Victor Griffin since kindergarten, and even then he knew how to maneuver people until he got what he wanted. "More like a bulldozer. He keeps coming at her from every which way. Homegirl giggled last time I talked to her on the phone about him. When have you known Minette to giggle?"

"You've got a point," Bailey said as she ran a hand through her red-brown hair.

"He did wear her down, now didn't he?" Vancy asked, having recently learned that Victor had surprised Minette with flowers, chocolates, and butter toffee peanuts on nearly every holiday that Hallmark made a greeting card.

"Sure did."

"And you matched them up by clueing Victor in to Minette's weak spots—butter toffee peanuts being tops on the list, didn't you?"

"Something like that," Bailey replied.

She was not prepared to give up the goods on Victor's method of courtship, nor was she ready to tell Vancy that when Victor asked for tips she had been a willing accomplice. She wanted Minette to tell Vancy herself.

"Girl, don't get modest on me now. Tell the truth."

Bailey planted both feet on the heater-warmed floor. "I don't mean to brag, but I do know folks," she claimed as she fell one notch for Vancy's challenging bait.

Knowing she had a strand of Bailey's ego by the root, Vancy cackled like a backyard hen. "Brag my butt. You glow whenever you hear those two are together."

Bailey's voice cozied up to Vancy's ear. "Speaking of together, I can't wait for you to meet Ridge Williams."

"Ridge as in mountain spine? Or Ridge as in soap opera hunk?" Vancy could not believe the brother's first name.

"Vancy!"

"Girl, I just can't believe I'm letting you fix me up."

"I'm not fixing you up exactly," Bailey denied in a teasing way. "I'm fixing dinner."

Vancy tossed back the last of her carob coated raisins and wished she had more. "In a pig's eye," she managed to say as she studied the carob crumbs in the jewel-cut glass canning jar she kept under the service counter. It sat beside the teddy bear cookie jar.

"Yours," Bailey countered. "We're full circle."

"Come again?"

"The word pig, as in pigheaded. That's you."

"Goodbye, Bailey."

Bailey laughed because they both knew Vancy was not about to hang up. "You just think about all that good soul food I'm gonna be putting my foot in for you tonight."

Vancy chuckled. "With your foot in the food and my butt on the line, dinner ought to entertain everybody involved."

"That's what I figured too."

Vancy squinted her eyes as she imagined the smug look on Bailey's face. "I just bet you did. What about the girls?" Bailey's daughters, Fern and Sage, often attended dinners hosted by their parents in their spacious home.

"Sam's parents are taking them to the carnival." The traveling show was all Fern and Sage could talk about.

Fern's friends, Jordanna and Cambria were tagging along for the festivities.

"Those two make dynamite grandparents," Vancy admitted wistfully.

She wondered briefly if she would have children for her parents to dote on someday. Even though her parents had divorced nearly a decade before, they kept in close contact with all their children.

"We love them dearly," Bailey replied, once again waving her toes before the electric heater. "So do the girls, now stop changing the subject."

"Umph," Vancy uttered with a bit of sarcasm, "and I thought I was slick."

"Thought is the word," Bailey teased her unorthodox friend. "What will you wear?" she asked with bated breath. "I heard you wore spandex to a recent baby shower."

"Something outrageous," Vancy promptly replied, fully intending to stir things up at the dinner party.

"Such as?" Bailey inquired, getting the message her friend was not going to make her matchmaking plans very easy.

But then, she remembered, there was not much that was easy about Vancy. She trusted few people, and those people she did trust she was loyal to for life. Bailey counted herself fortunate to be part of that small, select inner circle of Vancy McKay's goodwill.

"I'm wearing sequins."

"At an informal dinner party?" Bailey questioned, though she tried to keep her voice from rising with indignation. She had never known Vancy to be without a quirk in her attire. She was a beautiful, unusual, hard to forget woman.

"You're right," Vancy acquiesced, "I'll wear scarves."

"Vancy!" Bailey said as she bolted up in her kitchen chair. She didn't doubt for a second Vancy owned an outfit made solely of scarves, an outfit better suited for a colorful

belly dance performance than a casual dinner party between eight friends.

"Okay, okay, I'll come as a fortune-teller," Vancy said,
very pleased with Bailey's gasp of shock.

"Ex-homicide detectives don't go in for fortune-telling,"
Bailey responded, thinking Vancy just might succeed in
scaring the ever practical, ever logical former detective off
to different pastures.

Ridge possessed the right looks and brains to catch the
woman of his dreams. Bailey just wanted to make sure he
laid eyes on Vancy during the course of his hunt for a
lifetime mate.

"Told you I'm slick," Vancy crowed.

"Not slick," Bailey countered with little satisfaction. She
loved her friend and wanted a full, rich life for her. "You're
scared."

If Bailey had not struck a sensitive nerve, Vancy might
have laughed. "Girl, please," she muttered instead, wishing all the while she had devoured her stash of raisins
more slowly.

Heart-to-hearts with Bailey gave her the munchies, perhaps because she associated food with her oldest woman
friend. Bailey started cooking in their seventh grade home
economics class and had never stopped.

"You're as scared as Minette," Bailey softly declared,
knowing both women had once been hurt deeply by the
men they had loved. Neither woman was in a hurry to
expose themselves to that kind of relationship again.

"So what?"

Vancy could not remember a time when she and Bailey
did not get down to the bones of the problems and main
events in their lives. Over the many years of their friendship
they had learned to treasure the honesty flowing between
them, even when that honesty rankled tender nerves.

Bailey gently encouraged her friend. "Dinner doesn'

hurt. There are no strings, just a casual grouping of on-the-ball peers, nothing more, nothing less."

Vancy chuckled, thinking Bailey was as tenacious as a goat. "Exactly how long is your nose Pinocchio?"

Bailey laughed along with her. "Long enough to sniff out a love match or two."

"What does Sam think about all your matchmaking business?"

Bailey recalled him saying a lot of things about leaving affairs of the heart alone. She boiled his precise opinions down to one line, "He says not everybody wants to play *The Dating Game* or *The Love Connection*."

"See," Vancy chortled, "smart man."

Bailey took the intended barb with grace and humor. "Smart for marrying me."

Vancy lit a wand of jasmine incense, savoring the wonderful, holistic scent. "Girl, you're so crazy."

Bailey switched off the portable heater, then jammed her feet into worn leather loafers. Settled into her seat once more, her legs crossed at the thigh, she said, "Enough about me, Ms. Sidetracker. Are you really coming to the party dressed as a fortune-teller?"

"Yep."

"How about that slinky red dress?" Bailey suggested, her tone hopeful.

Vancy fiddled with the telephone cord and wondered what color to paint her nails for dinner, a color besides red; maybe purple, she adored purple. "Which one? You know how much I love red."

"The backless dress that makes you look like a runway model."

Vancy's husky cackle came to life once again. "Girl, you're so full of it."

"Wear that dress and Ridge will be full of it, too," Bailey announced, her tone matter of fact and straight down to business. A tall woman, Vancy maintained a beautiful, athletic figure that looked excellent sheathed in clinging fabric.

"Full of what?" Vancy asked, enjoying her conversation immensely. Bailey never bored her or made her wish she never called.

"Lust!"

Vancy almost fell off her chair laughing. "Stop before I bust the seams of my purple stretch pants."

Bailey grimaced at the immediate vision. "Purple?"

"Purple."

"Good grief, Vancy. Do you ever wear anything conservative?"

"Not if I can help it, why?"

Bailey placed a manicured hand to her furrowed brow. "Well, Ridge is rather . . . uh, what's the word I'm looking for . . . uh—"

"Lord, girl, don't tell me the man's a walking brown suit," Vancy loudly interrupted. She took her feet off the stool to plant them firmly on the purple throw rug beneath her seat.

"Something like that."

"But you said he's like Sam!" Vancy wailed.

Bailey spoke patiently. "I'm talking personality, Vancy, not looks."

Vancy considered her dinner party outfit. She would wear the biggest gold hoop earrings in her jewelry box, she decided; gold bangles, gold anklets, plus rings on her baby toes. "So he falls into the homely but nice category?" she asked, her voice a bit hushed as she broke her own thoughtful silence.

Bailey laughed outright. "Not hardly."

"Short then."

"Not even close."

"Uh oh," Vancy said, throwing her head back and closing her eyes. "He's bald."

"Now you know darn well that bald is stylish these days."

"I bet his front teeth are gold."

"Vancy, you need to lay off those B movies," Bailey advised, sounding exasperated.

"Leave Foxy Brown and Cleopatra Jones out of this," Vancy said in defense of her Sunday afternoon pastime, watching old flicks.

"That's what I'm telling you. Gold teeth. Vancy, you're too much."

"That's why I'm dressing as a mysterious fortune-teller for the dinner party tonight." When Bailey gasped she added, "A fortune-teller in silver sandals."

Bailey groaned. "You're wearing red, Vancy. You always wear a red dress to dinner parties so you stand out in the crowd."

"I'm changing my M.O. just for tonight."

"M.O.?" Bailey asked, her nose scrunched up to match the scowl on her face.

"Modus Operandi, meaning method of operation."

"I know what it means." She wanted to know what it meant when it applied to Vancy.

"You should know what it means after the mystery adventures you've been into with Sam. It all started with that suicide scandal over Mary Lou Booker."

"Poor Mary Lou," Bailey responded, thinking of her friend falling overboard on a pleasure cruise ship several years before.

"And then Sam ran into trouble with those skinheads."

"What a way to end the summer."

"You and Sam are the only couple I know who've had those kinds of adventures. Now that's what I want."

"Your own murder mystery to untangle with the man you love?"

"No, I want a little drama and intrigue, minus the murder of course."

"You're crazy."

"Well, breaking up with Raymond changed the way I

feel about everything. He's the number one reason why I've changed my M.O. The next man that wants to get next to me will have to get past some heavy artillery. If he's still standing when I'm done with him, I'll give him a chance."

"I've got the perfect man for your maximum level man test, which is basically to shock his socks off with your weirdness turned on turbo."

"Now you're talking."

Bailey was challenged. "Good, tonight will test my best M & M skills."

"M & M?"

"Matchmaking."

Vancy went for all out honesty. "I know you mean well by inviting me over to your house as a friend to meet a friend. I also know you've got too much ego to hook me up with a loser."

"I'll pretend that's a compliment."

"But for the record, I'm not too keen on this pretend-dinner-but-it's-really-a-matchmaking-thing."

"Forget the dinner thing, come for dessert."

Vancy ran the tip of her tongue across her bottom lip. She tasted carob. "I do love peach cobbler."

"I'm not talking about the cobbler. I'm talking about Ridge."

"Oooh Bailey," Vancy chastised, her eyes flying open from her peach cobbler daydream. "You've got no shame do you?"

"None, which is at least part of the reason why we've been friends since the sixth grade. Only the shameless, or shall I say, the adventurous girls could keep up with you. Besides all that, Vancy, life is too short to let good people pass you by."

"I'm not passing you by."

"You're passing up Ridge."

Vancy leaned her elbows on the service counter. "Okay

snoop sister. I'm just picking at the man to get your goat for meddling in my business. Truth is, I'm curious."

"That's no secret. Some single women look forward to meeting an eligible man on their best friend's recommendation, but no, you and Minette have to be picky and troublesome."

Vancy laughed. "That's right. We can't go out with every Tom, Dick, and Harry our married girlfriends send our way. Besides, the older we single women get the more picky we get. Both Minette and I are stable women with strong heads for business in this town."

"Braggart."

"The shoe fits, honey, and I do like to wear it. Now tell me a little bit more about this ex-detective."

"He's stable. You're flighty."

"Hey!" Vancy hollered, not liking the word flighty.

"Ridge is grounded. You're spirited."

Mollified, Vancy sniffed. "That's better."

"Ridge is territorial. You're adventurous."

"Sounds like trouble."

"Ridge is organized. You're not."

"Hey!"

Bailey tsked. "Do you or do you not keep your cash receipts in a cookie jar?"

"Okay, okay, so I'm not organized. Go on."

"Ridge is observant. You're sensitive."

"That's interesting."

"Ridge is a thinker. You're a doer."

"I sense a conflict coming on."

"Until he quit the police force, Ridge was a workaholic. You're not."

Vancy turned thoughtful. "I admit I'm interested, but you've only shown how incompatible we are."

"I don't think so."

"Why?"

"You each have what the other is missing," Bailey answered, not believing for an instant Ridge and Vancy would not make a smashing couple despite their different ways—if only she could get them together. Ridge was as reluctant as Vancy.

"People need similar strengths, too," Vancy stated from experience.

Bailey added fuel to her matchmaking cause. "You both are confident."

"I know I am," Vancy said in a smart-alecky way.

"Arrogant."

Vancy grumbled. "Give me a break."

"You both are forward thinking. You plan ahead."

"Go on."

"You drink chamomile tea to relax. No coffee."

Vancy liked that about the man she would soon meet. "Chamomile you say?"

"I say." Bailey answered, all smiles and good wishes. "Told you I know what I'm doing. You always said that a man who drinks herbal tea instead of coffee is worth a second look."

"Trust you to remember the off-the-wall remark."

"Yeah, trust me."

"Trust you to make trouble and call it dinner," Vancy countered, suddenly looking forward to meeting the former homicide detective.

Bailey said with a satisfied chuckle, "See you at seven."

About the Author

Shelby Lewis lives in Northern California with her husband, Steve, and their young sons, Steven and Randal. An avid mystery and romance reader, Shelby enjoys black and white movie classics, flea market treasure hunting, baking, and lazing at the beach.

Look for these upcoming Arabesque titles:

February 1997
INCOGNITO by Francis Ray
WHITE LIGHTNING by Candice Poarch
LOVE LETTERS, Valentine Collection

March 1997
THE WAY HOME by Angela Benson
SOMETHING SO RIGHT by Layle Guisto
NIGHT AND DAY by Doris Johnson

April 1997
HIDDEN AGENDA by Rochelle Alers
CONSPIRACY by Margie Walker
SOUL MATES by Bridget Anderson